IN CONTROL

THE SHORT, KINKY, OTHERWORLDLY FICTION OF M.CHRISTIAN

M.CHRISTIAN

ISBN 978-1-957863-35-1

Second Edition 2024
Parisian Phoenix Kink
ParisianPhoenix.com

"Alice" and "Gertrude" also appeared in
Juicy Bits: Erotic Stories of BDSM, Kink & Fetish
ISBN 9781957863184

Cover illustration: Liubov Mahda, istockphoto.com

Originally published by Renaissance E Books/Sizzler Editions, 2013

CONNECT with M.Christian:
www.mchristian.com
mchristianzobop@gmail.com

CONNECT with the publisher:

Substack:	parisianphoenixpublishing.substack.com
Web:	www.ParisianPhoenix.com
Facebook	@parisianphoenixpublishing
Instagram:	@ parisianphoenix
LinkedIn	@parisianphoenixpublishing
Patreon	@parisianphoenix
TikTok	@parisianphoenix
Twitter:	@parisbirdbooks

"M.Christian is the chameleon of modern erotica. One day punk,
another romantic; one day straight, another totally perverse and
polyamorous. But always sexy and gripping."

— Maxim Jakubowksi, editor of the *Mammoth Book of Erotica* series

"M.Christian is a literary stylist of the highest caliber: smart, funny,
frightening, sexy — there's nothing he can't write about ... and
brilliantly."

— Tristan Taormino, writer, speaker, sex educator, and activist

"M.Christian's fiction has a sexy logic all its own. He's inventive and he's
irreverent. His language can seduce, surprise, and body-slam you.

— Cecilia Tan, author and founder and manager of Circlet Press

"Reading these tales is like climbing on for a sexual magic carpet
ride through different times and places, diverse bodies, and infinite
possibilities."

— Carol Queen, author, sex educator

"M.Christian's erotic stories are always surprising, satisfying and
imaginative. The variety of his sexual scenarios is awesome, yet there's
an element to each that always rings authentic and true."

— Marilyn Jaye Lewis, author of *Neptune & Surf*

"M.Christian is a writer who takes you for a long walk down a dark
wet street at midnight. You can't get much more edgy and still be legal.
His fiction never disappoints."

— Nancy Kilpatrick, author of *The Power of the Blood* series
and *In the Shadow of the Gargoyle*

"M.Christian weaves sex in and around engrossing tales of odd
characters caught up in unusual — even bizarre — situations.
No quickies here, but fine reading that sizzles."

— Marcy Sheiner, editor of *The Oy of Sex*, and the *Herotica* series

CONTENTS

INTRODUCTION: DISCLOSURE

I've written a lot of things over the years: gay erotica, lesbian erotica, bisexual erotica, all kinds (of every kind) of fetish erotica … plus a smattering of romance, science fiction, horror, fantasy, and even non-fiction.

But, recently, a friend of mine said something that stopped me dead in my authorial tracks: "Why don't you write about what turns *you* on?"

To be honest, I've always been a bit … *resistant* to writing about myself. Part of it comes from the fact that I consider my sex life to be what I guess you could call *sacred*: a cherished time shared between me and the person I happen to be playing with. I've always thought that writers who — and this is not meant as an insult … or not too much of one — who sell their own sex lives on the page to be profiting from an intimate sharing of desire. Another part, I freely admit, is that for all my writing and sex-ed teaching I'm still a bit shy when it comes to being out about what honestly, truly turns me on.

But, thinking about this, I had a freeze-me-in-my-tracks revelation: I actually write a *lot* about myself.

Take this book, for instance: a collection of some of my short fiction — a lot of it with a BDSM kink: pretty much every story here is a part of me. Yes, the details may not be exactly *me*, but the emotional side of things — the important side as anyone who really understands about sexuality — is pretty much as intimate as you can get: "Alice" is the giddy nerves that comes with telling a lover what turns you on, "Moving" is about finding that special someone you can drop your guard down with, "In Control" is the fretting that arrives with the next day, "The Tinkling Of Tiny Silver Bells" is the glorious feeling of unquestioning love, "Dust" is the beautiful tears of being forgiven, "The Waters Of Biscayne Bay" is the liberation in the enlightened joy of a lover loving another person, *Painted Doll* was all about the tearing-of-the-heart from being too many miles away, and the sample chapter from *Brushes* is all about the pleasure that comes from giving pleasure … and so on and so forth, with just about everything I've ever written.

When I teach erotic writing I talk very much about this: that the details aren't really important, that the best way of reaching out to anyone, no matter what you are writing, is to dig down deep and put down, onto the page, your own emotional truth. Like a lot of teachers I simply forgot to listen to my own lesson.

So here are some stories I sincerely hope you'll like … for, like when I spend time with a lover, it gives me immeasurable pleasure to put a smile on another person's face.

–M.Christian

ALICE

It started with the laundry — how ironic is that?

Laundry was a kind of blind spot for Al. Ask him to take out the garbage, drive five hundred miles to help out a friend, weed the back yard or cook (he made a mean-ass clam chowder he was particularly proud of) and it would get done so quick and so neat that jaws would drop and eyes would pop. No muss, no fuss: just a well-executed chore or perfectly performed task.

But ask him to do the laundry, and by the grudging production he made of the whole thing — stripping the bed, picking up crumpled piles of clothing, hauling baskets downstairs, stuffing the washer — you'd think he'd been asked to give Karl Malden a sponge bath.

At first, Jeannine hadn't been bothered by this quirk.

"Just the usual breaking-in stuff," she'd thought to herself and told friends who asked about the couple's experiment in living together. "Nothing to worry a war-crimes tribunal about."

Four months later, she'd begun to think, "Okay, this is starting to really bug me," and clench her smooth hands into tight, white fists. Six months in, she was debating with herself how best to dispose of his body.

She had to be honest with herself and admit that he tried. But somehow, his trying only made it worse. Huffing and puffing like a kid asked to eat his broccoli, he'd make such a big deal out of doing laundry that Jeannine didn't know whether to make him stand in a corner or give him a Golden Globe for acting. Even when Al seemed to want to do the laundry, earnestly "helping out around the house" on her birthday, or when he'd done something spectacularly dumb and needed to do some housework Hail Marys, it didn't work out. Her favorite red dress, white shift, the linen, even a suede jacket went in — and what came out went straight to Goodwill.

Despite Al's laundry issues, he and Jeannine had it pretty good: Al's underground comic, *The Snitch*, was doing remarkably well — well enough that he didn't need a real job yet. Jeannine's store, Deco Mojo, was paying for their rent and a little more. Unlike a lot of their friends, they'd been together a little over a year with no sign of impending breakup or nasty drama.

In all their time together, including the months before cohabitation and after making the big leap into it, Jeannine and Al had a pretty cooperative relationship: some gives, some takes, fair play all the way around. Al did the shopping this week, Jeannine the next. This month Al paid the phone bill, next month Jeannine did. Except for the issue of the laundry, they kept everything fair and even between them.

That's not quite true, though. Everything was fair and even except for the law when it came to laundry and one other situation: the bedroom.

* * * *

But that's also not quite true — mainly because for Al and Jeannine, the bedroom was only one of the places where you fucked around. The Outdoors, you see, did it for Jeannine. The more out the better, especially when there was a real risk they'd get spotted by someone — extra-especially when they could be spotted by more than just one someone. Parking garages, baseball games, movie theatres, hiking trails– they'd tried them all.

Al called it "eye-porn." The way Jeannine reacted to being watched was like the way guys reacted to looking at anything and anyone sexy. He loved it almost as much as Jeannine did: crawling up the fire escape to the roof, giggling and whispering like schoolkids, laying out a blanket on gravel still warm from sunlight, a kiss, more kisses, clothes off, hands roaming, cock very hard, pussy very wet, fucking long and slow, then hard and fast knowing that someone could be looking at them any second or that hundreds — maybe thousands — were doing just that already.

But what did Al like? She didn't know.

"I'm not complaining, mind you," she said to some of her friends when they'd she and Al had first moved in together. "Not at all."

Four months later, "I just can't figure him out" was the order of the day.

At six months she was wondering what terrible secret he was hiding, what skeletons he had in his closet.

Then, one lazy Saturday afternoon — chores completed, laundry carefully ignored — they curled up together on their plush, painfully bright orange sofa and flipped through mail, stopping in the middle of bills and miscellaneous flyers to glance at the Victoria's Secret catalogue.

"Wow," Al said, brown eyes wide as Jeannine flipped through the glossy pages. "Pretty."

The times they'd gone to the museum and snuck in a quick blow-job amongst the French Impressionists, all Al had said was, "Nice." When they went to friends' gallery openings and fucked ferociously in the grimy bathrooms, all Al said was, "Eh." "Good" was what Al called his world-renowned chowder, and how he described their sex life. In all their months together, Jeannine had never heard Al call anything else by that one word of praise. Until, that is, page seventy-nine of the Victoria Secret catalog.

That night, Jeannine smiled to herself. It was time, she thought, for Al's skeleton to come out of the closet. Time, with the dreaded laundry, for him to come out — and play.

* * * *

"Perfect. Absolutely perfect. Or else," Jeannine said, uncomfortable with even the idea of a threat — but obviously excited by it.

"Or else?" Al said, as uncomfortable as she was with the threat — and just as excited.

"Or else you're going to be very intimate with some of my more intimates, Al. Do you get me?"

Al was speechless. But his face said what his voice couldn't.

"Good. Now, let's get it all done right, Al: fabric softener, the right temperature, no mixed colors, no running, nothing wrong. Perfect. No mistakes, Al." She cast him a cool glance. "I'm going out for a few hours — got some store stuff to take care of — and when I get back, I expect the laundry to be done like it's never been done before."

Then she went out, with a wide, wicked smile on her lips.

* * * *

"Let me see," she said, four hours and some-odd minutes later. "Show me what you've got."

"Ah, sure — " Al said, nerves making him hesitate, stammer. "Sure thing, babe."

"Don't call me 'babe' — not yet, at any rate. Now show me. And this had better be good."

"Yes — " he said, and started to address her as something that began with 'b' but caught himself, substituting a quick "be right back" and a smile.

The first basket was full to overflowing with sheets, pillow cases, blankets, and towels. Jeannine tried to keep the smile off her face as he pulled out each neatly folded bundle. Creases almost made her giggle with joy, seams made her flash some pearly white teeth — but she fought to keep her face stony and firm.

"Now the next one," she said.

The next basket was packed with slacks, jeans, blouses, socks, boxers, bras, shirts, and panties. Al may have screwed up every other attempt at laundry, but this time he gleamed, shown, sparkled, was absolutely spotless: she may have barely kept the smile from her face before, but now it took every once of control for her to keep from laughing and giving him a big hug — and the laundry had nothing to do with it.

She had to find something wrong, though. That was the game, after all.

"What's this?" she said, holding up a pair of panties.

"Um, er — it's your … panties."

"That's right, it's my favorite pair: soft, pearlescent, pure white with the frilly waistband and the tiny blue flower right in the middle. Right there. See the flower? But there's something about this flower, Al — something very, very bad."

Al swallowed hard but didn't say anything.

"You see, Al, my favorite pair of silky panties has four little green leaves next to that sweet little flower. Four. Not two, not three, not five — four. Now, Al, I want you to take these and tell me how many little green leaves there are next to that so-sweet little flower."

Al took the panties in suddenly moist hands, turned them carefully until the little flower faced him. Just as Jeannine had never heard Al use the word "pretty" before — not at the museum, not in a gallery — she'd never really seem him hold something reverently before.

"Three," Al said, glancing up from the panties to look her in the face. His eyes were wide and gently moist.

"That's right, Al. Three. Not four — three. One of my flowers is missing. That's not a good thing. Not a good thing at all. I asked you to do something and you didn't do it. I'm afraid, Al, that you'll have to be punished."

Al's face lit with a soft smile. "I understand." He seemed to want to add something else (Ma'am, Sir, Mistress, something like that) but didn't know what to say — yet.

"Good. Now strip."

Al's smile grew, took on a sweetness and a subtle 'thank you,' and he did as he was told.

Next to one of the baskets went his hurriedly unfolded shirt, shoes, pants, socks, and underwear, until he stood in front of her, tall and lean, all long bones and tight muscles, and very, very hard.

Jeannine looked at his gently bobbing cock. It took a lot of control not to reach out and stroke it, suck it.

"Very good," she said, her voice catching in her throat. She doubted she'd ever seen him as hard. "Very, very good. Now, Al —" she tossed him the sheer panties "— put these on."

At first Al didn't do anything. He just stood in front of her, very hard, with a strange expression on his face. Later, when she had time to really think about it, Jeannine would realize that among the emotions that were zapping around inside her boyfriend's mind — desire, suspicion, shame, fear, to name a few — the one that finally won out, that made him reach down and put one foot, then the other, into the satin undies and slowly, sensually draw them up his body, was relief.

"Very nice," Jeannine said, surprising herself at her own sincerity. He really did look … not pretty, but definitely very sexy: his very hard cock tented the white material like he was trying to shoplift a javelin, and the sheer material was already growing damp at the end with pearly pre-come. Again, it took all of Jeannine's control not to just lick the end, taste the salty bitterness.

"Very sexy, Al — no, that's not right. You're not really Al, are you? Not right now."

Al hung his head slightly, pulled his elbows and knees in, shrinking, getting younger, the rough and tumble Al fading away as Jeannine watched.

"Alice?" Jeannine said, the inspiration like a small shock. "Your name is Alice. Isn't that right … Alice?"

Al — no, because her boyfriend was gone. Alice, her girlfriend with the white satin panties, very big clit, and very small boobs, nodded slowly, happily.

"You're very pretty, Alice, in nothing but your white panties. Very sexy. Do you feel sexy, Alice?"

Alice smiled radiantly, saying wordlessly: Yes, very much so.

"Turn around, Alice. Show me your sexy little body. Show me what you've got, slut."

Alice chewed a thumbnail, eyes wide and moist.

"Do it, Alice — or do you want me to be upset?" Jeannine wanted to laugh, to cry, at how excited they both seemed to feel. It wasn't a game she'd played before — and never would have thought about playing with Al — but with Alice it seemed right, natural, and most of all, way too much fun.

Alice's eyes grew even wider. Then, slowly, shyly, she turned around, giving Jeannine a hesitant view of her boyish body.

"Very sexy," Jeannine said, suddenly aware of her own wetness. "I really like you in my panties. In fact, I think you look even better in my panties than I do. They're yours now."

"T-thank you," Alice said. Even her voice was soft and almost innocent.

Jeannine leaned forward and grabbed hold of Alice's huge clit in a powerful grip. Alice was startled, but Jeannine hung on and wouldn't let her pull away. "You forget your place … Alice. Do you want me to be displeased?"

"N-no," stammered Alice, hands falling to Jeannine's. Touching, but not trying to pull them away.

"'No, what? Who am I, Alice? What do you call me?"

Alice's face burned bright red. Her lips quivered but no words came out.

"Say it, Alice — or I put you to bed without any supper."

"Mistress…" whispered Alice. Then, with a bit more force: "Yes, Mistress," like a weight had been lifted.

"That's right. I'm your Mistress. Don't you forget it, either."

She let go of Alice's clit. The thin girl took a half step back in response.

"No — no, Mistress, I won't forget," Alice said, composing herself.

"You'd better not," Jeannine reached out and ran her fingers up the length of Alice's very hard, rhythmically flexing clit.

"So beautiful —" she said, almost a whisper.

Shaking her head slowly, as if to clear it, she said in a louder voice, "Now then, slut. Where were we? Oh, yes, that's right. You were giving me a show. I like a good show." Jeannine leaned back as if to inspect her new plaything. "Why don't you show me how hard that clit of yours really us. Rub it for me, stroke it through your new panties. Do it. Do it now."

"Yes, Mistress," Alice said, her voice honey and all manner of sweetness. Palm down, she dropped one hand down to the front of her panties and slowly started to rub herself.

"That's it," Jeannine said, gently parting her own legs in response, as if Alice's clit was somehow connected directly to her own. "That's it."

"Thank you, Mistress," Alice said, her eyes glazing over in pleasure.

As she rubbed, stroked herself, the front of her panties got wetter and wetter. Soon, the pale material was almost transparent, giving Jeannine a perfect view of the thin girl's monstrous clit.

"Thank you…" said Alice.

"Oh, yes, you slut. You love this, don't you, slut? You love it, being the nasty little girl, putting on a show just for me. Yeah, that's it; rub it, rub that sweet clit for me. Make those panties nice and hot and wet and sticky. Stroke it for me, stroke it…"

Alice bit down on her lip, her breath coming in shorter and shorter hisses until, finally, she didn't make any sound at all but her body tensed as if a kind of wonderful voltage slammed through her. She went rigid, locked tight in a shuddering orgasm, the front of her panties suddenly soaked with her sticky juices.

In a barely controlled fall, Alice dropped down first to her knees and then face first onto the carpet. She lay there for a long time, her body quivering and quaking with release, breaths now heavy and slow.

"Very, very good, slut," Jeannine said, reaching up under her simple skirt to hook a thumb into the waistband of her own, everyday panties. "That was quite a show. Quite a *nice* show. I'm very impressed."

The panties came off, soaked through. She tossed them aside.

"In fact, come here, Alice," she said, her voice a husky whisper, "and taste how impressed I am."

Slowly, weak only in body, Alice got to her knees and moved over to Jeannine until her face was parallel with Jeannine's downy pubic hairs.

Now it was Jeannine's turn to really smile, as the game got even better for her. Leaning down, she parted her plush lips, giving Alice a view of her very wet folds and pulsing clit.

"Taste," she managed to get out before her voice completely caught in her throat.

Alice did. Alice did, indeed. Nuzzling up between Jeannine's strong thighs, she flicked her tongue over Jeannine's clit. Hard and fast, slow and soft, Alice licked. Jeannine, standing above her but at that instant miles way, moaned and bucked, dipped and swayed, in response.

Finally, the pressure Alice was applying peaked and Jeannine cried — her version short and sharp and loud compared to Alice's near-silent and long — and she slid down, landing hard on the floor at Alice's feet.

Her body still working, she threw her hands around Alice, her girlfriend, and Al, her boyfriend, and cried hot tears of pleasure and wonderful discovery.

* * * *

Some stories really do have happy endings. Al's comic work continued to do well, receiving both critical acclaim and financial success. Jeannine's store became a hallmark of the neighborhood. Al and Jeannine, and Alice and Jeannine were very happy together — and their whites were whiter, their colors brighter, than ever before.

MOVING

"Don't move," she said.

"That's it?" I said.

"That's it. That's it, *exactly*. Don't move."

"Right now?" Smiling.

She returned my smile. "Right now. But get comfortable first."

"Isn't that sort of counterproductive?"

She tapped the tip of my nose. "Comedian. Don't worry, you'll get an experience."

"But not a moving one, eh?"

The smile stayed, but her words were serious: "Great experiences are always moving — but not vice versa. Not at all."

At least Sylvia's basement was warm. No, not a basement. Dungeon. That was it, though I couldn't think of it that way.

"Dungeon"— that was bricks, rats, iron bars, and the *Man in the Iron Mask*.

Who was in that, anyway, Lon Chaney? Errol Flynn? Jose Ferrer? I'd have to look it up later.

"Dungeon" certainly wasn't a basement rec room in the Avenues, the perpetually foggy ocean side of San Francisco. No bricks, no iron bars, no rats, at least not as far as I could see. But that's what Sylvia called it, so that's what I should've called it, too.

Golden-yellow, close-cropped, shag carpeting. A heavy table covered in black leather. A pine chest with a latch and padlock, closed and locked. It wasn't anything Lon Chaney, Errol Flynn, or Jose Ferrer would have been scared of.

But I wasn't Lon or Errol or Jose, or even Brendan Fraser, and I'd be lying if I said I wasn't nervous. It wasn't that I didn't trust Sylvia, but this was more than a bit new.

Sex had always been about a cock (mine), tits, and pussies. Not whips, chains, and "Yes, Mistress." But that's what it was for Sylvia. At least she understood my trepidations, thus the padlock on her terrifying war chest.

What am I doing here?

It wasn't the first time I thought that, walking in the door to her place. The response remained the same: because this was part of her life, and I wanted to be part of her life, too.

But there was something else — *bing!* — right there in front of my face. Sure I wanted to stay in good graces with Sylvia, but there was something else as well. Face it, I told myself, you want to see why this isn't a rec room but a dungeon.

You want to get it.

"Ready?" she asked.

"Rip roarin' — to do absolutely nothing, that is," I said, smiling as always.

"Get comfy. You don't want to cramp up." In a bow to my nervousness, she wasn't wearing her BDSM gear, the leather and latex she'd showed me in the dark depths of her closet, but instead a comfy yellow bathrobe.

Despite or because of it, she was still damned sexy: a beautifully full, round woman with deep night hair and flickering amber eyes and, looking at her, the last thing I wanted to do was play her game and the first to part her robe, cup her breasts, run a thumb over her nipples.

But a promise was a promise.

It was also hard — or rather I should say I was also hard — because she'd asked me to strip. Hopping up onto the table, my cock slapped back and forth against my thighs, and I tried to work myself into a comfortable position.

After a few minutes, I thought I'd found it.

"Okay, I'm all set — to do nothing."

"You said that," she said, tightening the flannel sash around her waist. "Now, look me in the eyes."

"Yes, Mistress," I answered, curbing the mischief I felt ticking my voice.

She frowned, and I felt suddenly, deeply sad.

"Don't say that unless you mean it. I'm serious."

"Sorry," I said, opening my hands in supplication.

She looked at me for a moment.

"Okay." She took a deep breath. "You do the same, a couple of deep, slow breaths: in, out, in, out. Think about your body, the position you're sitting in. If it doesn't feel good, then move."

I breathed in time with her, feeling my chest rise and fall. I moved my leg a bit, then my right arm.

"When it feels good, when it feels *right*, nod, and we'll start. It's a simple game: don't move. Try and keep the same position as long as you can."

"Hum .... how do I win?"

"Win? This isn't win/lose."

She kissed the tip of my nose, and I grinned despite myself. She looked thoughtful for a while.

"But you know, there *might* be a way to win, but I'm not going to tell you. You've got to figure it out for yourself. Now, you ready?"

What the hell was that about? I thought. "Ready as I'll ever be."

"Good. Now don't say anything, don't nod — don't move."

I didn't say anything, I didn't nod, and I didn't move.

There were rules. For something not a game, it seemed to have a lot of them. Breathing was okay, blinking was okay, involuntary movement was okay, though anything like a conscious twitch or jerk was out: Game over, thank you for playing, here's your complimentary Turtle Wax and a copy of the home game.

Thinking of that, it nearly ended before it began, images dancing through my mind of a 2.5 nuclear family seated down around a Parker Brothers game of domination and submission, spinning the punishment wheel.

"Oh, no, Bobby, drew the golden showers card..."

Sylvia, meanwhile, sat down on the chest and watched me. Looking at her, watching her watch me, another thought flickered through my mind. With a view like this, who cares about moving?

Distantly, I was aware my cock hadn't gone down. If anything, the sight of Sylvia seemed to increase the tempo of its gentle throb.

I blinked.

Then still looking at my lover, I wondered *what am I supposed to do now*? The rules of the game were easy enough, but what was the damned point?

Was I supposed to make Sylvia feel good by obeying her?

"Yes, Mistress; no, Mistress; right away, Mistress."

That could make anyone feel good, having a humble little slave — but what the hell do *I* get out of it — aside from a nasty cramp?

When I agreed to play Sylvia's game, I knew it could be weird, but, hell, I loved her — or at least I thought I did. But this part of her life baffled me, and after a minute of immobility, it still did.

But something niggled at the back of my stock-still noggin. I didn't want to be a pet, a slave, a subservient little twit who'd follow her around, wipe her ass, or who knew what. That pissed me off.

I wanted to move, say, "fuck this," get up, and walk away. It wasn't something I'd thought of when I'd agreed to play, but after a few minutes, my face started burning. I wasn't a "top dog" kind of guy, but I sure as shit didn't want to be a whipped one.

It led to me suppressing a cruel sneer: one finger, the one on the hand she couldn't see. She wouldn't know, but I would. There was something juicy in that: a little victory in our battle of "play." When the game was over, she'd think she'd won when I'd actually been victorious — and I'd smile a secret little smile at the expense of this big, bad, Mistress.

I felt the massage table's warm leather. I was sitting on the edge, a hand at my side where she could see it, the other behind me.

That one. The one behind. My left. Maybe the first finger, perhaps the second? The birdie digit I decided was too rude, too harsh for my invisible gesture of defiance.

Have you ever consciously moved your body, saying to yourself within the confines of your skull, "I am going to lift my finger"?

Take my word for it, working yourself like a puppet or an actor on the stage is *weird*.

I felt my hand, my finger (the first one, if you're curious), the muscles, tendons, tissues tense: all the wet, squishy stuff beginning to change from immobile to mobile. The will was definitely there, my body totally prepared — then something interesting happened.

By not happening. I didn't move, not at all, not even my finger. The room, which previously felt warm if not hot, became chilly, a parade of goosebumps running up and down my spine, arms, and thighs.

Why? Thoughts in my head, thumping together around like bumper cars, weird feelings, odd impressions — and something else. Have you also ever suddenly realized your body was doing something you *didn't* ask it to do, a part of yourself you normally have control over suddenly acting on its own?

My cock, you see, was hard — rock hard, steel hard, *very damned* hard. I'd been angry — and I never get hard when I'm mad.

I shrink, shrivel, deflate — you name it. Negative erection. But frozen for Sylvia, my cock was determinedly stiff. No, that's not right. I'd *been* hard (it perpetually, rhythmically pulsing against my thigh), but immobile for Sylvia, I became *incredibly* hard.

The entirety of my groin ached to sink that glorious hardness into Sylvia. Though I didn't move, I didn't let the slightest grimace of pain or desire show on my face.

Sylvia, watching, smiled and winked at me.

I don't think I'd ever been that hard — and I hoped I would be again. It felt like a deeply buried part of myself, lurking somewhere beneath my belly button, my guts, my soul was happy.

While above it all, among the creases and folds of my brain, something else rang loud and long.

Why didn't I move? Why didn't I get up and leave?

Because it's what you've always done. I heard my guts, my soul say in perfect harmony.

Goosebumps. Big, obvious goosebumps not that the words were spoken by an unknown inner voice, I'd had a psychotic break, or had been telepathically contacted by beings 'Not Of This Earth,' but what that voice said was *right*.

I liked to laugh, because everything below me seemed so inherently comedic. I giggled and guffawed at the world, seeing the billions and billions living on it– or who will ever live on it as suckers, idiots.

I didn't believe in *anything*, and even on the rare occasions when I did, I internally chastised myself for being another rat confused by a maze, a moron endlessly trudging on an eternal treadmill.

Lifting a finger, cheating at my lover's game was *so like me*. Anything serious, deep, possibly meaningful was a joke.

A joke on you.

I moved internally, not externally, dropping through layers of mind and memory. Pieces of myself floated by my consciousness: birthday traumas, schoolyard pain, relationship shames, adult disappointments … I won't go through them all, not due to the awkward intimacy, but in retrospect they are too damned dull.

I wanted to laugh, but not like I had before.

Muscles wanted to tug my face into a grin. Wanted though strenuously prevented. Peering inward, I'd realized I didn't have anything: gliding through work, avocations, even love while never getting close to anything or anyone.

My leg cramped. I fought to ignore it. Pain flared, a pulsing discomfort. I pushed it back, kept tightened muscles from knotting up. It was important, very important not to move.

Not at all.

What had I done with my life, nothing except years of hollowness periodically spiked with acidic laughter?

Someone I knew in college had written a novel, something I'd felt was pathetic, spending night after night working on something that'd probably never see the light of day or if it did, it'd vanish from the stands in a week or two.

Someone I knew in high school traveled the world, visiting the Dalai Lama in Berlin when the wall came down. I'd giggled that she'd spent all that money, used up all that time, and came away with nothing except memories and a few snapshots.

My lower back ached. It felt like a lead slug wrapped around my spine. I wanted to sit up, stretch, listen to the music of my bones realigning themselves.

I didn't. I didn't move.

I was bound. I was bound, so couldn't, wouldn't move.

What have you done? What have you accomplished?

Girlfriends thought I might kinda, sorta love. They'd wanted to talk, to think about the future. I wanted to have fun. How many had there been? One of them, a fun, little redhead named Cheryl, got married, and I laughed that she'd stood in front of her family and friends when more than likely she and her husband would talk to divorce sharks a year or two later.

What had I done?

The answer was not hard — I didn't want to say it, to think it.

Nothing. I laughed a lot, and that was all.

I wanted to cry. I wanted to cry like I'd never cried before. Self-pity roared, caught in an escapable trap.

I wanted Sylvia, who gazed at me with deep amber eyes, to hold me as my sorrows ran dry. I wanted her to make everything better because I trusted her, because I loved her.

I didn't cry. Crying was moving. I didn't want to screw up. I wanted to make it happen, to win this game. I wanted to feel good, and, with that, I wanted Sylvia to feel good about me.

I wanted her to know I could and would do this small, impossible thing she'd asked me to do.

Because she'd asked me to do it.

My body was a knot. Pain rolled through my muscles, tendons, and even — I swear — my bones. My cock remained stone, not deflating in the slightest during my inward voyaging.

Sitting there in bondage, I wanted to touch it, wrap my hand around it and relish in its simple, unquestioning hardness. I wanted Sylvia to see it, to admire it. I wanted her to take pride in it as she saw, for the first time in my life, I was trying.

Trying my best.

I will not move. I will not move. I will do this.

She sat there quietly, eyes moving over my unmoving body. I felt them like a physical touch, a warm caress soothing my cramped limbs.

Then there was a question in her eyes, and though I could put it into words, I knew the answer.

Yes. Yes, Sylvia, my love, whatever you require of me, whatever you desire, I'll do my best to give it to you — to give myself to you.

Did she feel me? Did she hear my silent answer? Her thoughtful half-smile never wavered as I felt that ghostly touch of her eyes again.

My legs hurt. My back hurt. My hand felt like it would never move again. My eyes were burning dry. My head swam, and for a heart-hammering minute filled with equal parts panic and shame, I thought I'd moved.

My cheeks felt strange. Had I failed? I didn't want to. I wanted to go beyond who I'd been.

My cheeks felt strange. I hoped I hadn't moved. I hoped, prayed, I hadn't moved.

Sylvia got up, walked towards me, the expression on her face new, unusual. I hadn't seen her like this before. I'd seen her laugh, cry, orgasm, sigh, be angry, but this was new.

Was this disappointment? Deep sorrow that I'd failed her?

I hoped not. I really, honestly hoped not.

Her hand went to my face, my cheek. The touch of her fingers was an electric jolt, and I felt my whole body would jump at the contact. But I didn't. I felt the come boiling up into my dick, ready to explode, but I didn't move, not an inch, not a little bit, not at all.

I didn't move.

"Sweetheart," she said, bending down to peer into my eyes. "Sweetheart," she said again. "Thank you, thank you so much. You've done what I wanted … and more."

Within her face was what I wanted, what I needed, what had been missing, what I'd given up on ever having.

Respect.

I slipped off the bench and into her arms, trembling all over.

"Thank you," I said, tears pouring down my cheeks. "Thank you, Mistress."

IN CONTROL

We met in the dark corner of an Internet chatroom. SLUTSLAVE, a nubile profile full of in-the-know vernacular with damned good typing skills, and MASTER017, my digital persona. We didn't really meet there, of course, but that's where we first started to talk. The dance was slow, at first. I've heard other doms say that they don't like it slow, sedate, careful — they'd rather snap their fingers and have them drop to their knees.

Me? I like the dance, the approach, the 'chat' in chatroom. Besides, I've had a few of my own snaps, the eager young slaves with sparkles in their eyes, and not a clue between the ears. Give me someone who knows what they're getting into. It's better, after all, to be wanted by someone who wants the best, as opposed to someone who just wants.

So we danced, we chatted, SLUTSLAVE and I — or at least that cyberspace mask I wore. Finally, after many a midnight typing, she complained with a sideways smile — ;-) — that she was looking for something where more than just her wrists got a workout.

Like I said… Step one, two, three, turn, step one, two, three. Careful moves in this courtship dance. No snap from me. I made her sing for her supper, pushing her along, not making it easy for her.

"Do you know what you're asking for, Slave?" I asked, clicking and clacking on my keyboard.

She did the same, and the dance changed its tempo.

"Yes, Master. I do."

We made a date to get together the next weekend.

* * * *

A knock on the door. Normally, even when it's expected, it can be jarring. Fist on wood. Bang, bang, bang! But not that night. I opened it.

"Welcome."

I had a picture, of course, and the flesh was just like it, though filled out in three-dimensional reality. Seeing her jarred me, but not unpleasantly, unlike the door.

"Thanks," she said with a smile, walking in.

I closed the door behind her. Full bodied, curved, somewhere between too young and too old, tight and firm from exercise. Eyes gleaming with sharpness, mouth parted just *so* with anticipation. Curly dark hair, her skin a Mediterranean patina.

We didn't have to say much, most of our negotiations having been done in emails back and forth. I knew she couldn't stay on her feet for too long (plantar fasciitis), didn't like metal restraints or canes. But her list of *yes* was longer than her list of *no*.

"Stand there," I said, pointing to the center of my wool rug. My room looked odd, with all the furniture pushed back, piled up: spare chairs on my big oak table, ottoman tucked underneath. The room was just the rug, a coarse wool bullseye, and my favorite plush wing-back.

"Yes, Sir," she said, the grin never leaving her lips as she walked to the center.

"Stop."

She did, turning slowly to face me. Her breasts were big, wide. Not a girl's, a woman's. Twin peaks on cotton fabric. No bra, as ordered. I reached out to one of the points, circled it slowly with a stiff finger. The smile stayed, but her breathing deepened, sped up.

"Did I tell you what to call me?"

"No –"

She hissed, trying to swallow a scream, as I pinched her nipple, hard. One of my *no's* concerned sound. My apartment had thin walls.

"Call me, 'Master,'" I said, low and mean, grumbling and growling, as I pinched even more.

"Yes … M-Master," she said, with a delightful stammer against the pain.

I released the pressure.

"Pain is your punishment. It will be frequent. Pleasure is your reward. It will be rare. I'm not going to ask you if you understand. If you didn't you wouldn't be here. Undress."

She did, sensually but efficiently. The white cotton dress came off first. Under was a pair of everyday panties, just white. No hose, only socks and shoes. As I had requested.

Lingerie doesn't interest me. Bodies don't even interest me. She didn't interest me. But what I could do to her — that was what interested me.

She was naked. Her body was good. Not ideal, but with a warmth and reality to her. Big, full tits with just enough sag to mean reality and not silicone or somesuch. A plump little tummy. A plump mons with a gentle tuft of dark hair. It wasn't a body that you'd hang on your wall, but it was a body you'd want to fuck. But that was on her *no* list, which was fine by me. I definitely wanted to fuck with her, just not with her body.

Her hands kept drifting up, a force of will keeping them from hiding her breasts, covering her nipples. I smiled. SLUTSLAVE had a modest streak. Priceless.

I got out my toolbag, my own kind of wry smile on my face. Other tops went on and on about their toys, pissing on each other about the quality of the leather, the weight, the evilness of certain objects. I sat back and watched them. Wry grin then, wry grin now. If I had a headboard, I'd have it carved: *a workman is as good as his tools*, it would say. *A great one doesn't need them at all.*

I added it up once. $50 was as high as I got. Show me any other hobby that could give as much pleasure as my little bag of toys — or as much wonderful discomfort to SLUTSLAVE.

I laid them out on the rug in front of her. I felt like a surgeon — or a priest.

"We're going to play a game," I said. "The rules are very simple. I ask a question. If you tell me the truth you get a reward, if you don't you get punished. Again, I won't ask if you understand."

I picked up a favorite, though to tell my own truth I like them all. This one was just the favorite of the moment. I squeezed, and the clothespin yawned open. I held it out to her nipple, which — I noticed — was nicely wrinkled, erect.

"Are you wet?"

"Yes," she said in a breathy whisper.

I could tell, her musk was thick in the room. I was hard. Hell, I was hard when I opened the front door, but hearing that, knowing that, my jeans grew that much tighter.

"First lesson. It's an important one. Sometimes even the truth can mean pain," I said, in my best of voices, as I released the spring on the clothespin, letting it bite down sharp and quick on her thickening nipple.

Her sigh was a lovely musical tone, a bass rumble of pain that peaked towards pleasure. Oh, yes, that was it. The first note of a long musical composition. Her knees buckled because of it, and I put a hand on her shoulder to steady her.

I kept it on for a mental beat of ten. Not long, but long enough. I released it, keeping my hand on her shoulder. It always hurts so much worse coming off than it does coming on. Sure enough, her knees buckled even more and she slipped, dropped down to my rug.

Still on her knees, breathing much more regularly, she looked up at me, chin level with my crotch. I knew if I said to, she'd unzip my fly, undo my belt, reach in with eager, strong fingers to fish out my dick, stick it into her hot mouth. She'd do it, I knew, but like the clothespin, it's so much better if you wait. So I did.

I stepped back, grinning at the flicker of disappointment on her face. You'll have to wait too, I thought. I retrieved my bag, and sat down in my chair, facing her. The clothespin was still in my hand and I found myself absently opening and closing it. A Dom's worry bead, I guess.

"Stand up. Right now."

She did. Her knees seemed a bit weak.

"Come closer."

She did, her gait slow and controlled. I reached down to my bag at my feet, picked up something new.

"You're mine. You belong to me," I said, looking into her face.

Her eyes shone, gleamed.

"I won't ask if you understand."

When I was a kid, I used to play with dolls. Well, maybe not 'dolls,' not exactly. No Raggedy Anns, no Barbies, not like that. I liked that they were mine, they belonged to me. I could make them do anything, at any time, and they didn't say a word. They just did it, forever smiling.

It was a new toy, another deceivingly simple thing. I saw it in some import/export place down in the city. Elegant and simple, black and glossy. Seeing it, I knew I had to have it. Having it, I couldn't wait to use it.

"Lean back," I said. I was tapping it against my palm, a lacquer metronome. Tilted back, her breasts swayed gently apart, just beginning to make that armpit migration. She was younger than I thought.

I ran the tip of the chopstick around her right nipple, feeling it skip and slide over her areola, the contours traveling down the length of it into my finger tips. She signed, softly.

Way back when, just after I outgrew those plastic dolls, I wondered if I had a dead thing. You know, preferring girls stiff and cold rather than warm and breathing. But that wasn't it. It wasn't them being immobile, plastic. It was me being in control, making them do what I want. Right then, she was my doll, my plaything, and I was completely in control.

I started tapping, steadily, almost softly at first. A smooth double-time. But after a dozen or so beats I moved it up to a harder, more insistent tempo. Her breathing quickened, started to grow close, to almost, maybe match my beats with the lacquered stick. I watched her stomach rise and fall, a background accompaniment, echo to her hisses and sighs.

I moved, circled her breast and nipple with my stick, painting her with the beats. Tap, tap, tap, sigh, sigh, moan, sigh. Then the other breast, but a little harder this time. She started to glow, shine with gentle sweat. I could smell her, a thick rutting musk. Now, she really was wet.

Now I tapped just, only her nipples. Each impact steady, sure, quick, and hard. She started to unconsciously twist her body, a little this way then the opposite, to get away from the beats.

For a moment, I thought about stopping. Make her stand up, make her get dressed, kick her out for such a show of life and independence, but that would mean throwing away and stopping my use of this lovely new toy. The stick as well as SLUTSLAVE.

Then, I did stop.

Time for the next movement. She lifted her head, looking long at me, breathing heavy and hard. Her eyes flicked with a bit of fear but more than anything, a plead: *More.*

Back into the bag. Simple. When you have control, you don't need gadgets, gizmos, fine leathers. Fifty dollars in the right hands, with the right toy, and you have all you need. I came up with a pair matching the first clip. Her eyes grew even wider, breathing deeper and quicker. She knew what was coming next. I didn't have to say anything.

The right one first. Instead, I leaned down and held it there, open, threatening around her so-hard nipple. She looked at it, then looked at me. Again, fear but more than anything a desire for me to let go.

So I did. Her guttural bellow peaked threateningly towards a scream. But she swallowed it and as she swallowed, she hissed and hissed it back into herself. I was impressed.

I kept the clip on. It was wonderful to watch it bob up and down with her steady, deep breaths. I could have watched it all day, thinking: "this is mine." This is mine. This is mine. But I had another tit to play with.

During all this, my cock had been confined, trapped in my pants. Turning to the other tit, I felt how very, very hard I'd gotten. But that would wait. I was in control here. Not my dick.

The other one. Again, I held it there, looming over a tight little point of nipple. Again, I let go.

This time a short, quick, honest scream blew past her lips. Sound was a concern, but frankly I didn't care. This was good, damned good. She was a good toy, a good plaything. She was mine to do with as I wanted.

I watched her, making sure the pain of the clips wasn't too much for her. She whistled her breaths, in and out, belly rising and falling as she tried to accept, flow with, use, and enjoy what was happening to her nipples, breasts, and body.

I liked to watch her, knowing that I was the cause of all this. Yes, my cock was hard — steel, stone, rigid — in my pants, but this was almost better. The bliss painting her body in shimmering sweat, making her pant and moan, making her clit twitch wasn't something of mine that could ever go soft, ever come too quick. I could make her come and come and come again and never take off my pants.

Time for the next step. Both pins were in place, both nodded, dipped and rose from their grips on her nipples as she squirmed against the pain. I picked up the chop stick again.

"See this?" I said.

She pulled herself up from her blurry rapture. Her eyes took a long time to focus. She looked. She nodded.

I tapped one clothespin, hard, sending serious shocks down through it into her already aching nipple. She squealed in shock, in endorphin delight. I did the same to the other, then back again. Back and forth. She was a wonderful plaything, a fun little toy. I enjoyed playing with her very much. Oh, the things we could do.

I glanced up at the clock. A qualifier of our time together rang in my mind. Just a few hours, she had said, to start. Time had flown.

"Listen to me," I said.

Her vision was almost lost against the waves of sensation, but she managed to finally see me.

"We're almost finished — for tonight that is. But before we do, I'm going to fuck you."

She frowned past what was happening to her nipples, her tits, her body, her cunt. My words reached through it all and created a worry.

Not good to have my plaything in such a state. Time to demonstrate that I am in control, that for her, I'm the boss, I'm the Master. She is just a toy, and toys have nothing, not even a worry.

I reached into my bag at my feet, pulled it out, tossed it at her feet.

"I said I'm going to fuck you. My dick, right there in front of you, is going in your cunt. Do you have a problem with that?"

She didn't. The smell of her, the grin that flashed on her gleaming face told me that. Her legs were already gently parted, the kind of reckless, unselfconscious display that only a plaything in the middle of a high-flying pleasure/pain/endorphin rush could have. She may have had a worry, but she was more a hungry cunt. A wet and ready cunt. A wet and very ready cunt with a rubber dick on the floor in front of her.

"Pick it up," I said, though I didn't have to, not really, "and fuck yourself with it."

She bent forward, picked it up. Parting her thighs just a bit more, she showed me her pink wetness. The bare thatch of hair that descended from her mons was matted and gleaming with juice. Her lips were already gently apart, swollen and ready for my store-bought dick.

I knew I could probably have fucked her with my own cock, or simply unzipped my fly and stuck myself into her hot, wet mouth. But that would mean I was flesh and blood, a man, and not the Master I really was.

A Master is cold, a Master knows what to do with a plaything, a toy, a doll. I knew what to do. That's what I lived for. That dominance, that authority, that control.

She slipped the dildo into herself, just an inch to start. Then out, then in deeper, with a slow twist. She bit her lip in concentration. She closed her eyes in bliss, lost to the pain in her tits and the cock in her cunt.

Kneeling on my rug, legs very wide, she fucked herself. The gentle part ended quickly. She was now really, strongly fucking herself. A soft foam rimmed her cunt where the plastic slicked in and out. Some of her pubic hairs streaked along the length on the outstroke, curled in on the return. The hiss that had been only from the clips on her nipples was joined by the deeper sounds of a rolling, approaching come.

I didn't know her that well, but a good Master knows the sounds, no matter the toy. I could tell that she could see it coming, could smell, taste it coming. Her breathing broke, became shorter, panting.

Now.

Right now, I thought as I bent forward and put thumbs and fingers on the pins. I pulled.

Her eyes snapped open, fear lighting her irises. This time, still without words, she didn't say *more* but rather *oh my god.*

I pulled.

Not hard, just enough to drag her orgasm out, draw it farther out. Her fucking had slowed, eased, but she was too far along to stop. She couldn't if she wanted to.

I didn't want her to. So she didn't. I didn't need to say it, she understood it: the language of Master to SLUTSLAVE. Her fucking increased, pushing herself back up to the precipice. It didn't take long for her to be looking down the fast slope to her come.

This time she said, without words, *now*.

Yes, SLUTSLAVE: *Now*.

The pins came off. Screw noise concerns. Her scream came from her nipples, her tits but also from her spasming, quivering, quaking cunt. Her come rattled her, making her shake, her head bob back and forth. Her legs, already tensed from holding her forward, collapsed, spilling her backward on my old scratchy rug.

I watched her. Her breathing, after a long while, eased to a regular, resting rhythm. Then I went to my bathroom, got a big fluffy towel and draped it over her. She didn't say anything, not even thanks.

I got her a glass of water from my kitchen, even put a little slice of lemon in it. She took it with gently quivering fingers. Drank all of it, handed it back.

Then she said, "Thanks," but for the glass or the evening I didn't know.

Slowly, she got up, started hunting for her panties. I helped her, handing them over to her. She seemed to be happy.

Finally, she was dressed, though she looked funny with her hair messed.

"Are you okay to go home?" I asked her, my hand on her arm. "Should I call you a cab?"

"I'm — whooo," she breathed, laughing for a second with a shivering after-feeling. "I'm okay. Really. Thank you," she finally said. "That was a blast."

"I'm glad. I'd love to do it again sometime, soon."

"So would I. Really."

Her hand was on the doorknob.

"Write me," I said, holding the door open for her. "Send me a message and we'll pick a date."

"That'd be fun. Sure."

She walked down the hall. When she got to the end she turned, waved to me. I waved back.

* * * *

I checked my messages an hour or so later. Nothing. I watched some television, something I barely remember. Cops, I think. Or doctors. Something like that. Before I went to bed, I checked again. Nothing.

I sent her a message: "Hope you had a good time. Write when you get a chance."

In the morning, nothing. I browsed some of the chat rooms, even though I'd never known her to be there that early. Nothing, of course.

When I got home from work I checked again. Spam. A few messages from some friends. Nothing. She's just busy. Things happen, I told myself, not believing my own thoughts.

Before I went to bed I wrote another message. But I didn't send it. Maybe in a few days, I thought.

I checked again the instant I walked in after work. Nothing. Nothing at all.

I wrote her, against my better judgment. Simple, direct: "Concerned about how you're feeling. Please write."

That will do it, I thought. That'll reach her. Was it too much to ask? I thought she had fun. I thought she did.

But when I went to bed there was nothing but more spam, a few other messages. Nothing from her.

Around midnight, late for me, I went to bed. Nothing at all. I tried to masturbate but it didn't work out.

Eventually, I fell asleep.

In the morning I checked again, first thing. Nothing. Nothing at all.

I never used the handle MASTER017 again.

THE TINKLING OF TINY SILVER BELLS

Jasmine died two years ago. She showed up three weeks ago. Should have expected it, knowing Jasmine as well as I did.

I didn't know she was back, not really, for almost a week. Stomping around my little Long Beach bungalow, the one she had called my shell, I caught glimpses of faint reds, gold, of the hazy glow of sunlight through baggy tie-dyes, and of God's Eyes turning in the windows. They were just there enough so I knew I saw something, but was always a part, always a fragment of that something. Same with smells: incense, patchouli oil, pot, cheap wine, and that simple lemon perfume. Same with sounds, walking from the little kitchenette into the living room I would catch the slap of leather sandals on the hardwood floors, the opening clap of *Stairway*, and that tiny sound, that special sound that would always mean bells on toes. Jasmine.

She had outlasted the ghost of the Sixties by a few years, Jasmine had. Even though she'd been born in '71, she was a spirit of the Merry Pranksters, of Airplane, of the Summer of Love, acid, pot, Fat Freddy's Cat, the Stones, and tie-dyes.

It wasn't easy being a flower child in the age of the World Wide Web, ecstasy, coke, NIN, Courtney Love, and body piercings, but Jasmine pulled it off. She drifted with a smile on her face, and those fucking bells on her toes, through life, hitching rides with only good people, taking only the best drugs, being friends with only good people. She was a ghost of the Sixties, a spirit of the Haight and the Diggers.

Now, she was just a spirit.

I never could figure out how she could exist. She was fascinating in the same way a Mary Keene painting (admit it, you've seen them–big eyed children) can be: innocence distilled to the point of being surreal. Jasmine could hitchhike with Jeffrey Dalmer and get out alive, and with some money to help her on her way. Deep down, though, I knew her luck couldn't last. Whatever is out there hates the lucky and the innocent.

If there was a sin in Jasmine, in her perfect fortune, this unblinking good luck, it was that it didn't leave much room for depth or brains. Jasmine was a spirit who walked slowly through life, letting it bump her this way and that. Never ask her to meet you anywhere, never make plans around her. Jasmine was pot and incense and a soft, warm body that fit so comfortably in your arms, but she wasn't someone you could count on. No one who knew her said it, but we all knew it was true—and having her turn up two years after we all put her to rest in the Long Beach Municipal Cemetery proved it. She was late for her own funeral.

I can't really remember the first time I met Jasmine. Maybe it was that party to celebrate Rosie getting her first gig at the Red Room. Maybe it was that picnic that Robert and Steve threw down at the remains of the old Pike. Maybe she had just shown up on my doorstep like she always seemed to, jingling her tiny silver bells and lazily sweeping her tie-dye skirt back and forth. No place to sleep that night and Roger Corn was always up, awake, and willing to take her in.

God knew what we had in common, save we . . . fit somehow. We didn't talk music (Airplane! NIN! Joplin! Love!) or books (Kesey! Coupland!) or anything else for that matter (You're always so damned happy! What do you have to feel sad about?), we just fucked and played and took our respective drugs (Coffee & weed! H and Pot!). A spirit of the Sixties and one hack writer making his bread-and-butter writing porn, *True Detective Stories*, and articles on how to get your cat to use the toilet. We just seemed to go together somehow. We tolerated each other because we liked to fuck and kiss each other. Relationships can be based on worse things.

When I got that call, with Rosie so calm and collected, I was sort of ready for it. Jasmine always did what you expected her to, if you understood her, so when the phone rang and Rosie said that Jasmine had "passed on," I knew almost exactly how, where and why.

The funeral was sparse and sad for the little spirit, just the four of us. We had all pitched in to get the coffin. It was a colorful affair, you had to give it that: Rosie in a gaudy color-blast of a red sequined gown and boa, Robert in his own retro Seventies platforms and polyester, Steve with his beads and a (where the fuck did he score that?) Nehru jacket. I wore something aside from black. It was hard to find, but I managed to score a brilliant red shirt from a friend of mine. In many cultures, my shitty education not enough to tell me exactly where and who, red is the color for the dead.

Two years later, she was paying me a visit.

The first time I realized that something was going on I was scared shitless. I was washing my coffee cup (my lucky one), high a wee bit from this shitty Mexican that Rosie had scored for me, and I felt someone behind me. Thinking it was Montezuma's revenge acting through the weed, I shrugged it off.

Then, someone put their arms around my waist and hugged my little pot belly. I screamed, dropped my cup (*Java is the Spirit of Creativity*) into shards of ceramic, jumped into my Docs and ran over to Steve and Robert's.

You'd think that ODing on H in Rosie's apartment would be enough to keep a girlfriend down.

After a day or so, Rosie had convinced me that it was just lack of sleep, too many sips from my favorite mug, and a sudden flash of missing Jasmine. Rose said she felt her own late ex touch her sometimes, when she was in just the right mood. Of course there are differences between a dyke who'd gone off a bridge on her Harley and Jasmine the flower child overdoing the nostalgia just a bit.

Back in my place, I kept seeing those flashes of Jasmine's colors, smelling her smell, and hearing her bells. And sometimes, just before drifting off at three a.m. I'd feel her body warmth, just the heat of her at first, you understand, slip into bed with me.

About two weeks after that first touch in the kitchen, I was coming from the living room into the kitchen, empty new mug in hand (*Coffee is the Last Refuge of the Sleepy*), straight for my Saint Coffee machine and there she was: sandals, tie-dyed drawstring pants, simple white cotton shirt, scarf tied over her head. She was just there, at the kitchen counter, reading the paper, as I'd seen her a million times: joint burning in one hand, twirling a few strands of her blond hair in the other, chewing her lips at some newspaper headline or another. While she'd never actually said it, you could still hear her thoughts clear and distinct: *Why don't people get along?* Like she had on many mornings, as she had countless times.

And there she was again, after two years cold in the ground.

Then, she wasn't. She was there for about as much time as it takes to blink and think, for a panicked second, *is that really her?*

That was the first time. There were quickly others.

Jasmine liked to get in the bathtub with me when I was practicing my Death Trance Meditations. I like to sit in warm water with the lights off and think about myself in terms of flesh, blood, bone, hair and where all those pieces could end up, say, in a million years. You can get into some profound thoughts, laying in the dark, in the water, like that. And it can really mess with your head when the door would crash open and this demented hippie chick, all bounce and giggle, would come storming in jingling her tiny silver bells to pull off her balloon pants and squat herself down on the john to take a piss.

We used to fight about it, especially when I didn't even know she was in the house. You can imagine the shock she made after she was dead.

Mornings were Jasmine's favorite time of day. If I'd let her, she would go on and on about the opening of the day, with the accompaniment of birds singing and the soft applause of butterflies. She would wax cliché about the possibilities "dawning" (and giggling at the pun) with the new day and wonder how many adventures she'd have by sunset.

I am a Creature of the Night. I run from the burning rays of the sun and seek solstice in the cool darkness of my shell. But, still, I would always get up on a cheery blast furnace of a morning and be happy as a clam, especially when Jasmine treated me to one of her early-bird-special blowjobs. She liked that word, "Blowjob," said it sounded cute.

And, boy, was Jasmine skilled in its performance. Just the right amount of tongue, suction, lips, wet, dry, hands. She used to wake me up with soft kisses along my leg to let me know she was there and what she was up to. Then the kisses would run up to my stomach. A hand carefully placed over my cock and balls would warm them and add some sensation. When her mouth did finally touch my cock, it was after those soft, soft hands had stoked, teased, tickled and coaxed me into a painfully intense hard-on. Then, the mouth. Then, the real ride.

Mornings haven't been the same since she died. The sun must be a little brighter, stronger now. But then that one morning came. I was sleeping off my usual late-night writing stint (with a celebration of a new one finished: *I was a Teenage Trailer Park Slut*) when I got this amazing hard-on. I was so zonked that I really can't tell you if it was because of Jasmine or just because I was remembering my past with her, but there it was: long (no brag, but seven inches), strong and mighty. It was a mechanic's cock, a soldier's cock, a fuckin' basketball player's cock (okay, one of the white ones). I was proud of my cock, pleased with it that morning. With a hard-on like that, even hack writers can go out and become president (if you know the right people).

Then, Jasmine started to work on it. Dear dead Jasmine. Maybe because of my half-zonked condition, maybe because I just missed those lips, that throat, but I didn't do what I should have done– run screaming into that intense morning. But I didn't and dear dead Jasmine started to really get down and suck at my cock.

Death did not diminish her knowledge of blow-jobs, it seemed. She was all of Jasmine rolled into that one cock-sucking. I could, in fact, squint and see her as I had seen her on all those mornings. Her firm, slightly heavy body folded over, her face concentrating at my cock, with her right hand between her legs as she humped herself along with her sucking.

God, I could feel every inch of Jasmine, even if I couldn't see her. I could feel her tongue playing with the ridges and corona of my head. I could feel her lips play over my skin and veins. I could feel her throat, hot and firm, as I grazed it during her sucking. When I came, it was so good it hurt real bad. My come shot into an invisible mouth and vanished into ectoplasmic nothingness just as real-live Jasmine had liked to swallow it.

Other people would have run–to their pastors, to the cops (why?), to some science guys with a gizmo to exorcise the latent spectral energies, or to their priests (who would rattle their beads and speak some Latin). But most folks don't consider themselves a Child of the Night, grove on gloom, or hate any color save pitch black. Besides, Jasmine had been a sweet girl (tinkle, tinkle) and one motherfuckin' hot lay.

The fact that she was dead and haunting me didn't really seem to bother me at the time.

Jasmine was great for surprises. She liked to catch you unawares and get caught unawares herself. I can't remember how many times I'd "caught" Jasmine in the living room, or on the toilet, in my bed, rubbing one of her little, soft fingers up and down on her little moist slit. She was like a little kid in that, her body and other people's used to give her so much pleasure.

Death didn't even slow her down.

Listening to the newest *Lycia* CD, all moan, cemeteries, statues, clouds, rain, and mourners, I would get the strong impression of flowers, macramé, pot and the distinct sound of the tiny silver bells on toes jingling merrily away and look next to me to see Jasmine, half there and half not, not quite developed, not quite visible, legs spread wide, fingers gently rubbing up and down on her gumdrop-sized clit.

She became, over those weeks, to be more and more in my life. More so than she had when she was alive. Flesh and blood Jasmine used to come over maybe, tops, three times a week. Then, I wouldn't see her for months. Once a year passed before I walked in to see her dancing, naked, in my living room, the air thick with Mexican greenbud. But now that she had passed on, time seemed different to her. I would expect to feel or feel this spirit of Morrison, of Cream, of Sergeant Pepper at least once a day. Dancing in the living room, reading the Sunday paper in the kitchen, masturbating on the toilet, spooning with me in bed.

Bad? No, not at all. I felt special that of all the people she lived with, had fucked, had fought with, this one grungy hack writer living in a cheap-ass bungalow in Long Beach was the one she wanted to spend eternity with.

But there started to be other times, too. I would walk from the kitchen into the living room, coffee cup in hand, straight for my Macintosh with visions of *Truck Stop Bimbos* running through my head like a pneumatic chorus line. I would see her, standing by the window looking at something only the ghostly Jasmine could see. What bothered me more than anything was that Jasmine, alive, never really had an interest in the traffic on Oleander street. Jasmine wasn't just an echo drilled into me and my cheap-ass stucco walls. Something of the real Jasmine was here with the spectral one. Something that was missing something.

It became pretty obvious when she started to get *distracted* by things. Right in the middle of one hot and nasty morning blowjob, her ghost would stop right in the middle (*coitus spectoralus*) and I would get the definite impression that she was either looking out that window again like she was trying to remember something that she had forgotten.

Rosie, my only expert on dead relations coming back to cop a feel, got real quiet as she poured my Darjeeling tea, then said: "When Bolo left this world —" Rosie's ex who tried to jump her Harley from the Queen Mary to Catalina "— she came back to visit me a couple of times. It was like she just wanted to say good-bye in a way she couldn't when she was living. When she had done that, she just faded away."

"Yeah, but I don't get the vibe that Jas is here for a reason. It's like she just sort of moved back in."

Rosie stirred her tea with a chiming that reminded me way too much of Jasmine's tiny silver bells. "I got the impression from Bolo that she knew where she was going and that she was just stopping by. Remember, we are dealing with Jasmine, here. She could have gotten lost."

Great, a girl who could get lost in a Safeway had taken the wrong turn between death and the afterlife and was now trapped in my house.

It got worse soon after. The sex was still there, but now it was *sad*. The one thing the flesh and blood Jasmine wasn't was sad. The best way to get rid of her, in fact, was to get depressed. She'd vanish like pot smoke to find someone more cheerful. I've always had a hard time putting on a happy face, the one reason why Jasmine and I never stayed together for too long. Now, though, it looked like she was stuck in my dark little bungalow. Trapped.

And it was making her sad. It wasn't something she was used to, getting sad, and it was hitting her hard.

I heard her cry one day. I was hard at work on something for a porno mag specializing in dirty buttholes "and the guys who love to lick them" when I heard this weird sound. A sort of choking, wet sound. I hadn't heard it before.

I found her next to my bed, curled into a partially invisible fetal position. Jasmine was crying. It was that heaving, nauseous kind of crying, the kind you do when your cat gets run over, when you know you've taken way too much of the wrong kind of shit, when you're lost and know you can never find your way back.

I'm not a very altruistic kinda guy. I don't really know where it comes from, or doesn't. I just really don't give a flying fuck for a lot of folks. Yeah, I'll take Steve to the hospital when his T cells are low, or hold Rosie when she thinks too much of Bolo, but I don't really see those things are being good. Good is, like, helping fucking orphans or something, or giving change to the smelly crackhead who hangs out, or passes out, at the Laundromat. I don't have that kind of temperament.

I really didn't care that much about Jasmine. Yeah, I'd bail her out when she got busted for forgetting her purse and eating up a storm at some diner. Yeah, I'd give her whatever I had in my checking account when she really needed it. Yeah, I'd always let her in, no matter what was going on in my life. But she was just a pal, and a really good lay. I honestly didn't think of her in any other terms.

But then she was dead, and crying in my bedroom.

I could guess the cause. Bolo was a dyke who always knew where she was going and how exactly to get there. She was an iron-plated mean mother who knew what the score was–despite her profound depressions and mood swings. Jasmine was flowers and pot and the Beatles. She could get lost walking from the bathroom into the bedroom.

It wasn't all that hard, once I made the decision to do it. One phone call, to Rosie. Then into the bathroom.

I hadn't done my Death Trance since Jasmine had manifested herself those two weeks ago. It was just too much of a temptation for her and the shock of her walking in had been way too much when she was flesh and blood. Since she was a ghost, well, I don't really want to see if I'm cardiac prone.

Had trouble sleeping a few years back. I was lucky enough to have health insurance at the time, so was able to see a doc who could actually give me pills. I had only taken one. The fuckers were so strong that I stopped taking them and simply started staying up late.

I took five and laid in the warm water.

We are nothing but matter. We are nothing but the flesh that hangs on your bones, the blood that gushes through our meat. Bach took shits.

Aristotle got piss hard-ons. Mother Theresa, the runs. Ghandi really liked enemas. Lincoln got wind. We are animals that have learned to walk upright, that have trained themselves to use the next best thing to fishing with termites with a stick, the nuclear bomb.

I didn't have to think long. About the time I was drawing analogies between Sartre and seals that know how to play *Lady of Spain* on car horns, I was interrupted by a tiny sound, the sound of cheap Mexican toe rings chiming their tinny, cheap tones, the tinkling of tiny silver bells. Then, the sound of Jasmine pissing into the toilet.

But this time, it didn't sound mischievous. It sounded sad.

The pills had started to take effect. I braced my feet against the tub so I wouldn't drown and whispered, as loud as I could (which was just loud enough for the dead to hear), "Follow me."

I don't know what she saw, but I started to hallucinate pretty badly. Either the pills or I had really started to fade myself, I don't know. I was in the kitchen, full and real and solid, looking out my window. The sun was bright, so bright that I had to close my eyes against the brightness, but for some reason it reached right through my eyelids and right into my brain. I realized then that it couldn't be the sun, for at least the obvious reason that sun never came in that window, anyway.

No tunnel, no saints (or sinners, either), just that bright light. I felt myself start to come apart, like the flesh I had always talked about, thought about in my trances, was starting to unravel and decompose around me, leaving just a lightweight fragment of Roger Corn left. It wasn't a pull or an enticement, it was just a direction that I was walking myself to.

Jasmine. Somewhere I thought that, and reached back into my apartment for her, but I couldn't seem to find her. I looked in the bathroom (I looked so silly laying there in the tub, mouth hanging open), the living room, all the closets, the kitchen, *everywhere*. No Jasmine. Not even her ghost.

Then, that sound. Her sound. Cheap bells on her toes and a smile on her face. I found her masturbating in the bedroom, chubby legs wide and open, finger dancing on her clit. Typical. I smiled and took her hand and pulled her towards me, into me–

—and then pushed her away, into the brightness.

The cops and firemen busted down my bathroom door about that time. I don't remember much after except the sound of their tools smashing my interior door to cheap splinters. I probably don't want to remember being naked in front of all those macho public servants, having a tube run down my throat and having all that guck and pills poured out. Rosie had come through with perfect timing.

No repercussions, no real ones at any rate. What's another botched suicide, after all. At least I had accomplished something with this one. A spectral repercussion.

She's gone. You'd expect that. Gone wherever magical little Deadheads go when they OD. She's with Janice now, with Morrison and Lennon in a place where the Seventies never happened and where everyone gets along.

And, yeah, I hear those damned happy bells now and again.

BOB & CAROL & TED (BUT NOT ALICE)

"What are you afraid of?" Not spoken with scorn, with challenge.

This was Carol, after all. His Carol. The question was sweet, sincere, one lover to another. Really, honestly, what are you frightened of?

Robert fiddled with his glass of ice tea, gathering his thoughts. He trusted Carol. Hell, he'd been happily married to her for five years so he'd better, but even so, it was a door he hadn't opened in a long time.

They were sitting in their living room. A gentle rain tapping at the big glass doors to the patio, dancing on the pale blue surface of the pool beyond. In the big stone fireplace, a gentle fire licked at the glowing embers of a log.

Carol smiled. As always, when she did Bob felt himself sort of melt, deep inside. Carol, it shocked him sometimes how much he loved her, trusted her, loved to simply be with her. He counted himself so fortunate to have found the other half of himself in the tall, slim, brown-haired woman. They laughed at the same jokes, they appreciated the same ear of jazz, they both could eat endless platters of sashimi, and in the bedroom, the garage, the kitchen, in the pool, in the car, and everywhere else the mood struck them, their love-making was always delightful, often spectacular.

"I don't know," Bob finally said, taking a long sip of his drink (needs more sugar, he thought absently). "I mean I think about it sometimes. Not like I don't like what we do, but sometimes it crops up. A lot of the time it's hot, but other times it's kinda … fuck, disconcerting, you know? Like I should be thinking of what we're doing, what I want to do with you —" a sly smile, a hand on her thigh, kneading gently "— instead of thinking about, well, another guy."

Carol leaned forward, grazing her silken lips across his. As always, just that simple act, one sweeping kiss, made his body (especially his cock) stiff with desire.

"Sweet," she said, whispering hoarsely into his ear, "I don't mind. I think it's hot. I really do."

Bob smiled, flexing his jean-clad thighs to relish in his spontaneous stiffness. "I know. It just feels weird sometimes. I can't explain it."

"What do you think about? Talk to me about it. Maybe that'll help a little bit." Her hand landed in his lap, curled around his shaft. "Pretend I'm not here," she added, with a low laugh.

He responded with a matching chuckle. "Oh, yeah, right," he said, leaning forward to meet her lips. They stayed together, lips on lips, tongues dancing in hot mouths. Bob didn't know how to respond, so he just followed his instincts. His hand drifted up to cup Carol's firm, large breasts. Five years and she still had the power to reach into his sexual self, to get to him at a cock and balls level.

But there was something else.

"I think it's hot," Carol repeated, breaking the kiss with a soft smack of moisture. "I think about it a lot, really. The thought of you with… What was his name again?"

Bob doubted Carol had really forgotten, but he smiled and played again. "Charley. College friend."

Charley: brown curls, blue eyes, broad shoulders, football, basketball, geology, math, made a wicked margarita. Charley: late one night in their dorm room, both drunk on those wicked margaritas, Charley's hand on Bob's knee, then on his hard cock.

"We fooled around for most of the semester, then his father died. Left him the business. We stayed in touch for a year or so, then, well, drifted away. You know."

"I think it's wonderful," Carol said, smiling, laughing, but also tender, caring, knowing there was a Charley-shaped hole somewhere deep inside Bob. Carefully, slowly, she inched down the zipper on his shorts until the tent of his underwear was clearly visible, a small dot of pre-come marking the so-hard tip of his cock. "I think about it when we play. When we fuck."

Bob suspected, but hearing Carol say it added extra iron to his already throbbing hard-on. Carol normally wasn't one to talk during sex. This new, rough, voice was even more of a turn on.

Bob felt a glow start, deep down. Even to Carol, Charley was something private, but hearing Carol's voice, he felt like he could, really, finally share it.

"He was something else, Charley was. Big guy, never would have thought it to look at him. That sounds stupid, doesn't it?"

"No, it doesn't. You're speaking from the heart, sexy. Since when is anyone's heart logical or fair?"

Carol had gotten his shorts down, quickly followed by his underwear. Bob's cock had never seemed so big or so hard in his life. It was like two parts of his life had met, with the force of both working to make him hard, so damned hard. Carol kissed the tip, carefully savoring the bead of come just starting to form again at the tip.

He smiled down at her, taking a moment to playfully ruffle her hair before allowing himself to melt down into the sofa.

"I wouldn't call him 'sweet' or 'nice,' but he could be sometimes. He just liked … fuck…"

The words slipped from his mind as Carol opened her mouth and, at first, — slowly, carefully — started to suck on his cock.

"Fuck … yeah, he liked life, I guess. I don't even think he thought of himself as gay or anything. He just liked to fuck, to suck, to get laid, you know. But it was special. I can't really explain it."

Carol took her lips off his cock for a moment to speak.

"You loved him, didn't you, at least a little bit?"

As she spoke, she stroked him, each word a downward or upward stroke.

Bob didn't say anything. He just leaned back and closed his eyes. He knew she was right but that was one thing he wasn't quite willing to say, not yet. He'd come a long way, but that was still in the distance.

Carol smiled, sweetly, hotly, and dropped her mouth onto his cock again. This time her sucking, licking, stroking of his cock was faster, more earnest, and Bob could tell that she was aching to fuck, to climb on top of him and ride herself to a shattering, glorious orgasm.

But she didn't. Instead, she kept sucking, kept stroking his cock, occasionally breaking to whisper, then say, in a raw, hungry voice: "I think it's hot … not him just sucking your cock … but that you have had that. Bet sometimes … we look at the same guy … and want to know what he'd be like … to suck … to fuck."

Even though Bob was … somewhere else, damned near where Carol wanted to be, he knew she was right. It was hot, it was special, and he recognized that. He wanted to haul her off her knees, get dressed, and bolt out the door to do just that. The kid who bagged their groceries sometimes at the Piggly Wiggly, that one linebacker, Russell Crowe. Bob wanted to take them home, take off their shirts, lick their nipples, suck their cocks, suck their cocks, suck their cocks…

Something went wrong. With Bob on the edge of orgasm, Carol stopped. Bob felt slapped, like ice water had just been dumped into his lap. He opened his eyes and looked, goggle-eyed as Carol got up off the floor, straightening her t-shirt over very hard nipples.

"Didn't you hear that? Of all times for someone to ring the fucking doorbell."

* * * *

Tugging up his pants, Bob rehearsed what he'd say. Mormons? Slam the door in their faces. Door-to-door salesman? The same. Someone needing directions? "Sorry, but you're *way* off," then do the same.

Just as Bob got to the living room door, he heard Carol, who'd been a lot more dressed, speak.

"Ted! How's it hanging?"

Bob rounded the corner, a smile already spreading across his face. Of all the people to have knocked on their front door, Ted was probably the only one who would have understood.

Ted and his charming wife Alice lived just across town. Normally, Bob and Carol would never in a million years have crossed paths with them, but it so happened that Ted worked in the coffee place right across the street from when Bob worked. After six months of going back and forth, Bob finally struck up a conversation with Ted and found out, much to his delight, that the tall, sandy-haired young man and he had a lot in common: the Denver Broncos, weekend sailing, and Russell Crowe movies. Bob and Carol felt very relaxed and even sometimes sexually playful around Ted and Alice, even going so far as to having a kind of sex party one night, when they all got way too wasted on tequila and some primo greenbud that Ted had scored the night before. All they'd done was watch each other fuck, but it had been more than enough to blast Bob and Carol into happy voyeuristic bliss and fuel their erotic fantasies for weeks afterward.

"Low and to the right," Ted answered, smiling wide and broad and planting a quick kiss on Carol's cheek. Bob gave Ted his own quick greeting, a full body hug that, only after he finished did Bob realize had probably given Ted more than he expected with regard to Bob's still rock-hard dick.

Bob and Carol smiled at each other, feeling relaxed and still playful in the presence of their friend.

"Where's Alice at, Teddy? Somewhere in the depths of Columbia?" Bob asked.

38

Alice was the other half of Bean Seeing You, their little coffee house, and was often away trying to wrangle up all kinds of stimulating delicacies, not all of them coffee-related.

"Worse than that," Ted said, playfully ruffling his friend's brown locks. "Deepest, darkest Bakersfield. I'm kinda worried about her, the last expedition down there vanished without a trace."

Everyone laughing, more out of released tension than Ted's weird brand of humor, they retreated back to the living room and the couch. As Bob and Ted sprawled out on the couch while Carol got some drinks, Bob couldn't help but wonder if their friend had figured out that they'd been almost screwing their brains out a few minutes before. The thought of it made Bob grin wildly.

"Come on, bro," Ted said, picking up on the smile. "Out with it."

Suddenly tongue-tied, Bob was glad when Carol walked in with three tall, cool drinks. "One for the man of the house —" Bob "— one for the handsome stranger —" Ted "— and one for the horny housewife." Carol.

"Cheers!" she concluded, taking a hefty swallow of her own.

Bob and Ted toasted her, Bob almost coughing as he drank. The drinks were stiff and then some. He smiled to himself again as he sank back into the sofa. Talking about Charley made him feel like a secret had been released from some dark, compressed part of his mind. He felt light, airy, almost like he was hovering over his body, looking down at Ted — tall, curly-haired, quick and bright Ted — and Carol. Carol, who even just thinking of her made his body and mind recall their wonderful love-making.

Sneaking a furtive glance at Ted, Bob looked his friend over more carefully. In his new, unburdened vision, Ted looked … well, he wasn't like Charley, but there was still something about Ted that made Bob think of his college friend. No, his college lover. Something about their height, their insatiable appetite for life, their humor.

"Is it hot in here or is it just me?" Carol piped up, laughing at her own cliché.

Bob and Ted laughed, too, but then the sound dropped away to a compressed silence as Carol lifted off her t-shirt and theatrically mopped her brow. Bob's mind bounced from Carol's beautiful breasts, and her obviously very erect nipples, to Ted's rapt attention on them.

Bob was proud of Carol, proud that she was so lovely, so sexy. He wanted to reach out and grab her, pull her to him. He wanted to kiss her nipples as Ted watched. He wanted to sit her on the couch, spread her strong thighs and lick her cunt until she screamed, moaned and held onto Bob's hair as orgasm after orgasm rocketed through her as Ted watched. He wanted to bend her over, slide his painfully hard cock into her, and then fuck her still she moaned and bucked against him as Ted watched. He wanted Ted …

Carol's shorts came off next. Naked, she stood in front of them. Like a goddess, she rocked, back and forth, showing off her voluptuous form. But even though he loved her, and though she was probably the most beautiful women he'd ever seen, Bob turned to look at Ted.

Ted, with the beautiful Carol standing right there, was, instead, looking at Bob.

Bob felt his face grow flushed with … no, not with what he expected. It wasn't embarrassment. Dimly, Bob was aware of Carol walking towards him, getting down on her hands and knees again, and in a direct repeat of only minutes before, playfully tugging his cock out of her shorts and starting to suck on it.

Still watching Ted watching him — with Carol sucking his cock — Bob smiled at him. In Carol's mouth, his cock jumped with a sudden influx of pure lust.

Carol broke her hungry relishing of his dick.

"Bob," she said, "I really think Ted would like you to suck his cock."

Now, Bob was embarrassed, but not enough to keep him from silently nodding agreement.

"I'd love that," Ted said, his voice low and rumbling. "I really would."

"Take your pants off, Ted." Carol said, stroking Bob's cock. "I want to watch."

Ted did, quickly shucking his shirt as well as his threadbare jeans. He stood for a moment, letting Carol and Bob look at him. Bob had seen his friend's cock before, but for the first time, Bob really looked at it. Ted was tall and thin, his chest bare and smooth. His cock was big — though maybe not as big as Bob's (a secret little smirk at that) — but handsome. It wasn't soft, but it also wasn't completely hard. As Carol and Bob watched, Ted's cock grew firmer, harder, larger, until it stuck out from his lean frame at an urgent 45 degree angle.

"Bob," Carol said, her voice purring with lust, "suck Ted's cock. Please, suck it."

Ted crawled onto the sofa, laying down so that his head was on one armrest, his cock sticking straight up. His eyes were half-closed, and a sweet, sexy, smile played on his lips.

Bob reached down, turning just enough to reach his friend and not dislodge Carol from her earnest sucking of his own dick, and gently took hold of Ted's cock. It was warm, almost hot, and slightly slick with a fine sheen of sweat. He could have looked at it for hours, maybe even days, but with Carol working hard on his own dick, he felt his pulse racing, his own hunger beating hard in his heart.

At first he just kissed Ted's cock, tasting salty pre-come. With a flash of worry that he wouldn't be good, first he licked the tip, exploring the shape of the head with his lips and then his tongue. As his heart hammered heavier and his own cock pulsed with sensation, he finally took the head into his mouth and gently sucked and licked. Ted, bless him, gave wonderful feedback, gently moaning and bucking his slim hips just enough to let Bob know that he was doing a good job.

As Carol worked him, he worked Ted. They were a long train of pleasure, a circuit of moans and sighs. Time seemed to stretch, and distance compress until the whole world was just Ted's dick in Bob's mouth, Bob's dick in Carol's mouth — all on that wonderful afternoon.

Then, before he was even aware it was happening, Bob felt his orgasm pushing, heavy and wonderfully leaden, down through his body, down through his balls, down through his cock, and, in a spasming orgasm that made him break his earnest sucking of Ted's cock to moan, sign, almost scream with pleasure. Smiling at his friend, Ted followed quickly behind, with only a few quick jerks of his cock as Bob rested his head on Ted's knee.

Bob felt *good*, like something important, magical and special had happened. The world had grown, by just a little bit, but in a very special way. Resting on his friend's knee, Carol kissing his belly, he smiled.

Everything right with the world.

* * * *

Later, the sun set, and everyone very much exhausted by many more hours of play, Ted stumbled to the front door, with Carol helping him navigate through the dim house.

"Thanks for coming," she said with a sweet coo, almost a whisper, so as not to wake the heavily slumbering Bob in the next room. She kissed him, soft and sweet, smiling to herself at the variety of tastes on his lips.

"I was happy to. Very. Thanks for asking me to … come," Ted said, smiling, as he opened the front door.

Carol smiled. "Thank you for giving him such a wonderful gift. Next weekend then?"

"Definitely. Next time, I'll bring Alice."

Another gentle kiss, a mutual "Goodnight" and the door was closed.

THE HOUSE OF THE RISING SUN

Sunset: hot day melting into warm night. Amina stood, watching the shadows lengthen, feeling a heavy breeze pass her by, the hard iron balcony rail a stiff weight across her belly.

For a while she just looked at the people walking along the street below, calmly following their progress as they went wherever they were going. Not for the first time since Stanley had left her, she wanted to be one of them — any of them: a pair of Greek sailors; a young black man in threadbare jeans and a stained T-shirt, pedaling a wobbling, squeaking bicycle; a tourist couple in their pressed whites, standing out in their catalog-bought profiles; a fat man who didn't walk as much as slowly swim through the heavy sunset atmosphere, his legs seemingly linked by some internal arrangement to his fat arms swinging rhythmically by his side.

Many went by — 'til the sun had dropped behind the filigreed rooftops, and the street lamps started to, at first glow then burn brightly — but she sadly remained herself.

Finally the night touched, hinted at, becoming cool so she turned away from the iron curlicues of the balcony and walked across the small boarding-house room to robotically turn the antique light switch by the door. Yellow light snapped down through a dirty, cracked ceiling fixture, bathing the room in harsh realism: sink stained with a rusty high-water mark, mirror above cracked with an angry bolt, wooden floorboards that had been worn not into a smooth sheen but rather a broken and splintered forest. Wallpaper covered the walls, a tawny rainbow of mildew, and where it didn't — it had curled away from the soft plaster in stiff tubes and torn twists.

"Bathroom's down the hall, girl. That's why you be gettin' this one so cheap," the manager had said. A polished noir Buddha, she'd sat, rocked back on a low stool by the front door. A simple white dress, all lace and tiny red stitching, covered her great body. She was a momma, like a primordial soft bosomy comfort made into a breathing person. As she spoke, she'd cooled herself with a fan lettered with a gospel hymnal — too slow to deliver a good breeze, but too fast for Amina to see what it said. "But you be gettin' a sink, so you ain't bein' completely uncivilized."

Amina hadn't argued, and yet hadn't agreed, either. The red brick building across the street from the iron pickets of the cemetery had neither been her destination or even a way point. She been walking since dawn, a shocked somnambulation that had started with Stanley's note on the kitchen table, and ending with this big black woman calling to her: "Here, girl! Rooms for a tired lookin' lady."

Money had been exchanged. How much Amina didn't care. Not many thoughts inhabited her mind during that long walk, and even after she'd climbed the stairs under the simply lettered sign: Rising Sun. Only a few thoughts had managed to make themselves known to her as she'd leaned over the balcony — wishes to be anyone but Amina Robinson.

Then, as the sun set and the not-hot-but-warm night had started, she thought a few more. Not words, really, just a cool rationalization. She'd not brought anything with her. no razors, no gun, not even some pills. She was only two floors up, too low to jump. The ceiling fixture didn't look strong enough to support her, even if she had anything like a rope. The mirror was obvious, its sharp-edged cracks promising — even without a handy bathtub.

In the end, she retreated to the mildew-sink of the too-soft bed, old springs complaining as she settled into it, not avoiding the escape she so desperately wanted, but rather not wanting to face even her fractured reflection.

* * * *

Amina sat on the bed for a long time, listening with half an ear to the architectural mumblings of the old building: the hissing of water through pipes, the rolling creeks of footsteps next door and up above, the flapping of the shade in the open window.

Like an aching tooth she couldn't help tonguing, she replayed Stanley, hurting herself with his absence. Each act — the last fight, the daisies he'd brought home from work one day, the way he'd looked at her when she undressed in front of him, the color of his nipples, his laughter — seemingly to press harder down on her shoulders. She cried, after a time, but her tears were long since used up.

She couldn't go on. She knew that, felt the truth of it somewhere down deep inside herself, but — still — she sat on the edge of that bed in the House of the Rising Sun and did nothing, except weep without tears.

Night: warm darkness pushed back by street lights, diluted by flickering advertisements. The sounds of passers by seemed louder, as if the sunlight of only a few hours before had done its own kind of pushing back, their volume increased by its absence. Now free, their voices and the sounds of their cars, bikes, and trucks echoed up into the small room.

Amina stood and went to the window, intending to close it. She stopped, though, in mid-stride. *What did it matter?* she thought to herself in sentiment if not in those exact words. *I won't be able to hear anything very soon.*

Then, she did. Hear something, that is: a knock — thunderclap, pistol shot loud in the small room — and a voice: small, quavering, weak, helpless.

"Hello?" someone said from the other side of her door. "Hello? Can you hear me?"

She didn't have to. Still, she did. She turned, walked to the door, slipped the cheap chain, turned the knob, and opened it just so much.

"Thank god! I thought someone wasn't in here."

She was small, young — maybe 20 to Amina's 30, with hair as straight as dried pasta and as yellow as polished gold. Freckles dotted her pale cheeks, and her eyes were puffy and swollen from tears.

"Please, can I come in — please?"

She didn't need to, but Amina did. She opened the door wider. Stumbling over the first words in many hours, "S-sure," sounded like gravel pouring out of a coffee can.

"Thank you, oh thank you –" the young girl said, hunching down and moving quickly into the room.

Then she turned, and before Amina could do anything, had wrapped her thin, surprisingly warm, arms around her.

Wet tears seeping through her dress, onto her shoulder, Amina's arms moved without her. The girl was so slight, so small, putting her arms around her was like hugging a doll.

"I just — I just didn't want to be alone," the girl said. Then she repeated, as much to herself as to Amina: "I just didn't want to be alone."

Amina patted her warm back, feeling — distantly — the knots of her spine and the planes of her shoulder blades.

"I'm here," Amina said, without really feeling like she was.

"Can I … can I stay with you for a while?" the girl said, pushing herself back just enough to look up into Amina's eyes.

Amina still wanted to leave, just not be … there or anywhere else. But the girl's eyes, tugged at her, needed her. She didn't want to stay — in that room, in this world — but she also couldn't leave this sad, lonely girl, either.

* * * *

Midnight: the darkness still warm, the sounds of sunset and early night chased away by the weight of hours. Twelve, it seemed, was too deep, too black, to allow anything but a single wandering drunk who tried to sing — and failed — a song Amina didn't recognize.

Under the blankets they were warm. How they'd gotten there seemed so quick as to be part of a half-performed dance.

One step then another: "I just don't want to be alone anymore. Please, I just don't want to be alone." Then, "Thank you, thank you for opening the door. Thank you for being here." Her sobs had turned to shivers, and between her sobs she'd managed to slip, "Please, hold me close."

And so, in bed. Curled around each other under the thin blankets against a turgid breeze — shivering, ever so slightly until their mingled heat stilled the tremors.

Amina didn't speak. Instead, she stroked the young girl's yellow hair — a soothing motion that seemed to come from somewhere deep inside herself. She thought about saying something, the first real thoughts she'd had all day, but didn't. Words wouldn't have been enough — so, instead, she just stroked the young girl's hair.

The girl, though, spoke — or rather mumbled sleepily into her shoulder: "I don't want to be alone anymore — don't want to be alone. Hold me, please, hold me. Don't want to be alone anymore …."

Sleep started to tug at them, then pull in earnest. Before she was even aware of it, Amina's eyes closed and — to the soft, rhythmic breathing of the young girl, she drifted off.

She dreamed of Stanley, of a time when the two of them had rolled around on their tiny bed in the back of their little house. It was like a slippery body memory, the touch of Stanley's rough hands on her thighs, the weight of his hips on hers, the slight tang of beer on his breath, the slight burning of his stubble as they kissed. The way his sharp toenails occasionally grazed her ankles.

From this she drifted up, floating away from the dream and back into that warm, dark room. The girl, invisible under the blankets, was molded on top of her — the gentle weight of her small body pressing lightly down, pushing

Amina into the thin mattress. One of the girl's hands cupped Amina's right breast, her fingers calmly stroking the sides, delicately pinching her nipple.

Stanley had been a ferocious lover, a two-armed, two-legged thrust needing something to penetrate. When his lips found her nipples, Amina usually paid for this nurturing need of his with an even more vigorous than usual fuck — as if he was forcing his prick through herself and into his own weakness. A fuck like that was more a demonstration of his force than a need to come. After a time, Amina had feared his chapped, thin lips near her breasts and had taken to wearing at least a T-shirt to bed, and sometimes even a bra.

Sometime during the night the temperature had risen — and buttons had come unbuttoned. The girl's lips were too soft, too delicate. It was as if a hint, and not firm reality, was kissing — then sucking — Amina's nipples. The ghostly memory of Stanley's rough lips, flashed through her mind — then faded with a great surging wave of tingling pleasure. Even the deep reflexes of fear that usually accompanied any kind of contact with her nipples was stilled by the loving touch of the girl's gentle lips. With the wave, the swelling bloom of her body's response — nipples knotted, heart beating faster, breath shallower, muscles tightening, cunt liquefying — Amina found Stanley fading for the first time. A small tongue ringed her crinkled tips, and against her will, she found herself arching to meet the accompanying gentle suction.

It wasn't so much a girl's lips and tongue on her body — for Amina didn't really think of her in that way. In the darkness of the room, with the hole that Stanley's cruelty and departure had opened in her, it was just contact. Someone had looked down, saw the fragile, broken woman at the bottom, and had extended a hand down. Lips didn't matter as much as the thought of being seen, and desired — who it was incidental to that fact.

Distantly, through the hot, heavy haze of the girl's breath between kisses, between sweet nibbles, between sucks, Amina caught the falling bass note of a ship's horn sounding on the river. The reminder of the heavy waters of the Mississippi, the still-turgid atmosphere of the night air, made it seem as if she were floating in bath water, buoyed by the girl's touches on her body. The sucking, yes, but also her thin fingers dancing along her sides, the curves of her heavy breasts, the tension of her thighs, the gentle quakes of her calves seemed to lift Amina up, hold her above the bed, above even the sad exterior of the House of the Midnight Sun.

Squeezing her eyes shut against a sudden sharp peak of excitement, young teeth grazing her so-tight nipples as the girl's fingers playfully pinched at the underside of her tits, brought stars to Amina's eyes — completing the illusion of flight. Deep into a warm night, hanging above a vibrant tapestry of blue and purple starbursts, she floated on the girl's tender desire.

When those hands fell to the inside of her thighs, Amina parted them without a thought — save to be propelled higher into that starry canopy and away from the harsh earth, away from small rooms in run-down hotels, away from the pain of breathing, away from the pain of loneliness.

The first kiss was a lightning tear across that velvet darkness, a quick flash of desire that made Amina grit her teeth and whistle a breath. The first lick, the girl's tongue cautiously starting at the top of Amina's already wet cunt — just shy of her throbbing, pulsing clit — was a shivering rush through her body, a chiming that seemed to race through her. Toes to nose, Amina's body tensed and relaxed, tensed and relaxed to the accompanying strokes of the girl's strong, stiff tongue along her labia.

She crashed — down, down, down, through the ceiling, *wham!* into her body. Amina was a woman, on a smelly mattress, under a thin blanket, in a dive somewhere near the French Quarter with a girl she'd didn't know. Her legs were spread, her nipples were hard, and her cunt was very wet. She almost brought those legs closed to keep the girl away from her and the shimmering pleasure she was delivering. She even tensed in preparation, lifting a hand — feeling it drag and catch at the scratchy blanket — to put it on the girl's head, and half-formed the words *no, please.* But she stopped, hand only raised, legs only slightly tensed, words completely unspoken.

At first she didn't know what it was. Later, in the morning and days beyond, Amina would look back at that moment with some sadness (too long) and much joy (looking forward to more). But there in that little hotel, in the middle of a warmish night, it was just good. It was the best kind of good, a whole, pure, brilliant, good.

The moan escaped Amina's lips without permission, escaping from tension and loneliness — a long struggle that made its release all the more intense. Soon, the moan turned to gasps, which evolved into sweet murmurs — cresting once, twice, and more, many more times in more sharp cries, more deep moans.

What the girl was doing was a mystery. But Amina didn't care. She was there, in that sad hotel, on that warm night, under that cheap blanket, and she didn't care. She was desired, and — best of all — she was loved.

They came even faster after that, as if the way had been opened and the coming flowed through that opening in herself. With each, her liberation released her body, and her hands rubbed the girl's head between her legs, stroked her tiny ears, and allowed her legs to squeeze — ever so slightly.

How many was a mystery — one of many. In the end, she slept — the opening and the outpouring exhausting her. As she slept she dreamed, but on waking she couldn't remember anything about it — except she hadn't been alone.

Stanley hadn't been there, but she hadn't been alone.

✶ ✶ ✶ ✶

Morning: When she awoke, hard morning sunlight beating through the open window, the girl was gone.

The front door was closed, but just barely: a narrow seam of hallway showed between the thin wood and the jam.

Amina's dress was twisted and bunched. Standing quickly, she turned it, buttoned it, and smoothed it where it had crept up the cheeks of her ass.

Then she opened the door wider. The corridor was empty — quiet except for the muffled conversations of static-laced televisions talking to themselves. As she walked, then trotted, then ran towards the stairs, she wanted to call out, to cry the girl's name … and felt a deep tug down inside herself when she realized that she didn't know it.

The manager, the Buddha momma was outside, as if the black woman had not moved from her seat near the front door. As Amina trotted down the threadbare hall, the woman kept her rhythmic fanning — steady and undisturbed.

The street was just waking, slow pedestrians and the unearthly quickness of those used to the early hours. Faces approached and the silhouettes of bodies retreated but, standing on the narrow street, none of them was the girl.

"Excuse me," Amina panted, turning back to the big black woman, "but did you see a young woman go out? She was blond, thin — blue eyes …."

"Ah, girl," momma said, smiling, a pure beaming light of cheekbones, bright eyes, and a shimmering smile. "She's gone, she is. Been here long enough, but she's had ta got back ta where she belongs."

"Please, I want to find her. Tell me where she is …?" Amina said, hunger panting her words, making them sharp and forced.

"Girl, she be where she always be. She be where she come from," momma said, smile never wavering as she snapped her hymnal fan shut with a clap of rattan and paper. "She be where she be loved. You just be needin' to be shown that she there, is all. Sometimes you just be needin' to be shown how to be there for yerself, how ta love yerself."

With the fan, momma leaned slowly forward and tapped — one, two, three — Amina between her breasts, over her rapidly beating heart.

"If the lonely be bitin', you just look down here –" tap, tap, tap –"– and know that she be there. She always be there, girl, when you be needin' ta love yerself."

The day was starting. The city waking and starting to move around them. Smiling, leaning forward, Amina kissed the black woman on the forehead. Then she slowly walked off into the beginning of a day — the girl staying with her, keeping her company, loving her, with every step.

WATER OF LIFE

Except for memories, the big house was empty.

Claire's footsteps tapped down the hall, echoes bouncing back to her ears with shocking clarity. The upstairs bedroom: nothing but faded hardwood floors, the house's pervasive gently colored wallpaper, a window framing the gentle waving of willows in another summer windstorm. It hadn't been one of their rooms, but Gregory's presence filled it nonetheless. She remembered passing by the door one day, seeing a neat pile of art books next to the window, one of his thick notebooks flipped open to quick sketches in harsh charcoal.

She looked down the hall towards the master bedroom and paused. Too much there, too many memories flung into the haunted emptiness of the house. Rather than be visited by her lover's ghost, she paused at the door, then turned and walked back.

Down the stairs, the windstorm changed softly to rain, its tapping of raindrops the only accompaniment to her footsteps. In the main hall, a faded rectangle remained on the wall where Gregory's painting of wildflowers used to hang. Ghost wasn't right — Gregory was gone, but not to the hereafter.

The memory of their fights brought heat to her cheeks, the pain fresh even after a year. Her recollection of that last fight wasn't even clear, probably just another of their old fights: his art going nowhere, his resentment at being supported by Claire, her frustration with his on-again, off-again passions … one generic fight too many.

At the back door she paused, watching but not seeing the light rain start to fall. The garden was the best part of the house, an Eden surrounded by tall brick walls, a paradise in the midst of downtown New Orleans. Many people loved her home, its ornate ironwork, its elegant lines and ageless architecture, but her garden held them without words. Claire smiled, remembering a dinner party, friends in their finery, Gregory in jeans and sweatshirt; conversation tickling everyone into smiles, with a little help from champagne bubbles. She saw Gregory, standing there, looking so handsome and proud next to what she thought to be his best creation.

It was unlike him, which was why she probably liked it so much. When pressed about it, he'd dismiss the ornate fountain with a quick wave of his hand. He'd gone beyond such things now, he'd proclaim, and show her sketches of heavy, oppressive designs, and complex mobiles.

Hindsight can deceive though, and looking out the backdoor at the fountain he'd called "Water of Life," Claire wondered not for the first time if she really loved the elaborate sculpture or simply worshipped its presence. The house was empty of Gregory. He was gone. The only thing that remained was her memories, and the fountain.

* * * *

It bubbled. Tall, elegant, water spouted and flowed from its heights. Sometimes when Claire looked at it she thought it was a tangle of vines, a nouveau cascade of green iron. Other times, it was like water itself, frozen in the act of flowing over invisible stones, a Zen lesson cast in metal.

When struck by a bitter loneliness she thought it was like Gregory, unidentifiable and just about useless.

But, like her old lover, it was pretty. Graceful, it reached just above her bright red hair. It seemed to play music, a kind of water music that became a liquid sonata in the rain.

Despite the gentle downpour, she walked to it, the recklessness of the act making her feel alive after the ghostliness of the house. The first drops on her head were icy, then became almost warm in the humid night. Underfoot, the garden's brickwork patch was slick with wet moss under her bare feet.

It bothered Claire that she missed him so much. She knew it had been a stupid relationship. A matronly real estate agent and the young artist, like something out of a torrid romance. But it had been good, when it was good, and it hurt now that it was over.

Gregory hadn't been perfect, but he'd been hers. She knew she wasn't beautiful. She was getting older, her face showing merciless lines, and her body starting to recognize inevitability. She was middle-aged, and before

Gregory all she'd had to look forward to had been a slow slide into old age and invisibility.

She stood at the sculpture and missed him all the more.

In the warm summer rain it was wonderful, water cascading down from the top in soft bubbling streams. Flutes of rain twisted from the top, focused from tiny details. In the rain, the fountain seemed to come alive.

Standing before it in her simple white nightdress, she held her hand under one of the spouts, the heavy stream of water falling on her palm. Its relentless weight was like a patter of a heavy heartbeat, warm, soothing, almost living. Turning her body slightly, she boldly let it patter down onto her shoulder, quickly soaking her body in intimate moisture. She was shocked to feel her body respond beyond the water's cool temperature. Her nipples knotted tightly and her eyes glazed over, lost in concentration.

She thought of Gregory: firm, slightly callused hands on her body; the way he'd touch her, the special little voiceless rituals they'd had when they'd made love. The kiss above her navel, the ring of them around her nipples, the slow descent of his finger down the cleft of her sex.

Taking a deep, ragged breath she stepped further into the pounding water. It was like a parade of hands caressing her, touching her in ways that shocked, scared, and — most of all — excited her. As if by design, a stream of water now splattered against her right nipple, patting it into firm rigidity. Another stream, again as if especially sculpted for such a purpose, descended down from the twisting top of the fountain to fall with determined throbs onto her belly, from there (with delightful irregularity) onto her plush mons, and (with wonderfully frustrating irregularity) vibrated through that cushion on to her swollen clit.

Without will, her body began to twist and gently turn under the water flowing from the fountain. As if guiding the hand of a lover, she moved this way and that to let the water tap and pound at her nipples, neck, shoulders, belly, mons and oh, yes, deep within, her clit.

The water came down in a tireless performance. It came down, and Claire ...

The shock of what she was doing — standing in a now-thundering rainstorm in a soaking wet shift, excited beyond understanding — froze her, propelled her mind away from herself. There was no stopping her orgasm, which fought with brilliantly hot cheeks against the cool, glorious water. The body rush made her legs weak and her hands quiver, and her hand shot out almost without volition, grabbing the side of the heavy iron fountain.

A few deep breaths, ragged from the noises she realized she must have made, and her head stopped swimming. Reason, stubbornly, returned. She was standing, soaking wet, in the middle of the rain, in the middle of her garden, hanging onto Gregory's sculpture for all she was worth.

After a time, when her heartbeat steadied and her legs stopped quivering, she pushed herself off the heavy ironwork and stood, staring up at its elegant height.

Before turning and making her way unsteadily back to the house, she thought: I miss you, I miss you so much.

* * * *

The next day passed like a dream in a series of half-felt, disconnected events that, when she took a moment to think of them, didn't seem to make any sense. The office hummed with busy salesmen and empty conversations. Lunch was forcing tasteless food into her mouth while staring at the slow-moving green snake of the Mississippi. When Claire realized that she was especially watching the way the mighty river pushed itself against distant pilings, flowing with heavy sensuality around the strong timbers, she shook her head violently and took a big sip of her vodka and tonic.

The house that night seemed even bigger, even emptier. Against its shadows and echoes, she turned on every light and the two televisions. Sitting on the edge of her bed, still dressed in her work clothes, she closed her eyes and tried to imagine a party going on around her. The illusion calmed her, lifted her spirits, if just for a little while.

That night it rained again in a heavy downpour that sounded like thousands of feet running across the roof. She wanted to open the bedroom window and look down into the garden. She wanted to see the willows swaying, the puddles forming on the mossy bricks, and, more than anything, to watch flow and tumble from the sculpture.

Instead she went to bed early, and cried. Eventually, she managed to sleep.

* * * *

It was cool but not cold to the touch. It was surprising, as if she expected it to be chilled, and thus rejecting her. Maybe it was Gregory's skill, his craftsmanship, but a cynical part of her instead thought it was just her desperation.

Her hands caressed the flowing details: the spouts that could be leaves, or the necks of surreal swans; the shafts that might be branches of some kind of rippling tree; or serpents lurking as a metal sculpture in her garden.

Water bubbled from its what-might-be-spouts and tumbled with a delicious weight from its what-could-be-leaves. Running her hands through the liquid, she felt goose bumps sprinkle up along her arms.

Cold or anticipation? She didn't know, but she did know that she felt quite a bit of both.

She wanted Gregory, wanted his touch, the comfort of his smiling presence. But he was gone, her house empty.

Only his fountain remained.

The water tapped gently against her arm, like a precise massage. Feeling it, she felt her body give a deep, answering surge of desire. She couldn't have Gregory, but she could make a loving connection with what he left behind.

Her preparations had excited her, as if simply giving herself permission had started the coals. After she'd put on her dowdy but comfortable one-piece swim suit, clipped back her long red hair, and slipped on a pair of ugly little beach slaps, the fire had started. Walking out into the cool evening, moss sliding under her rubberized feet, the flames really started to build.

The water fell on her palm, then her arm. Its impact was soft and hard at the same time, a firm sensual cascade. Hypnotized, she watched the skin of her arm react to the pressure. It wasn't too difficult to morph the feel of the water falling on her into Gregory's hand gently tapping on her soft skin. It was as if he was with her again, but through a wonderful performance of his art.

Claire stood, letting the water descend over her body, relishing in its heaviness, coolness, sensual playfulness as it splashed and flowed, pattered, tapped, streamed over her body. A part of Claire's mind, uncomfortable with the idea of pleasure for its own sake, saw Claire standing under the streams of rainwater, the residue of the past flowing off her arms, washing away from her body, removing the pain of Gregory's departure with the water from one of his works of art.

Another deeper and more earthy part of Claire was simply enjoying this. Touch, even the elemental touch of water on her skin, was so sensual, and Claire's body certainly was responding.

Slowly, as if the water were filling an empty portion of herself, she felt her body warm with excitement. As before, the streams of cool, heavy liquid started to stir her body. Her nipples knotted. Down deep, she felt her desire liquify, growing into an almost painful need for more. She knew distantly that her own hot moisture was mixing with the thundering water churning from the almost-vines, could-be-swans of Gregory's fountain.

Answering the demands of her nipples, she caught the straps of her suit and in one simple motion, bared her full breasts to the downpour streaming off the fountain. Pounding on her sensitive skin, the water seemed to boil on contact with her heat. Opening her eyes momentarily, staring up at the green tower of the fountain, at the water churning and flowing from its fluted spires and twisted projections, she expected to see steam rising from her body, mixing with the light mist from the rain. She felt exalted, excited, and desired.

The water continued to splatter down on her, tapping firmly on her hard nipples and down between her breasts to tap gently again on her mons. From there it became a cool finger stirring around her clit.

As before, she found herself lifted up, supported by the cool sensuality of the water flowing from the fountain. As before, she felt her body hotly respond to the touch. Her mind started to leave her gently, flying high above her body, above the green tower of the fountain.

As before, she knew her joy was coming, pushed along by the shock of what she was doing as much as the water's touch. In a last act of will, she dropped her hands down to her plump thighs and carefully slipped a finger down to where her suit pinched upwards. There, with the water pounding onto her breasts and nipples, onto her shoulders and chest, she found the throbbing bead that seemed at that moment to be her entire focus of existence. All it took was half a dozen quick strokes, half a dozen tiny touches to push her that extra inch, to shove her over the edge.

When the orgasm came it was like a parade of electric shocks, a torrent of voltage up her spine. Again, she pitched forward to grab the edge of the fountain, but this time her legs weren't enough to support her and she fell on the slick bricks. She rested there, kneeling before the fountain, its water ceaselessly pattering onto her head and back, for what seemed like eons.

Eventually, her breathing slowed and strength returned to her legs. Walking back to the house, she breathed in out, in out, in out until the rasping in her throat subsided. Claire was shocked at how clear her mind was, how she felt at peace with the world. It seemed the water had done more than just wash away her loneliness. It had washed away a lot more.

Without sadness, she missed Gregory even more. It was as if his art had reached a part of herself she didn't know she had. With a flash of shame, she regretted everything negative she'd said about his work. The "Water of Life" proved that he was a wonderful artist with skills that awed her.

Looking back over her shoulder at the fountain, and the water playing on and around it, she thought again those words: I miss you.

It wasn't until she got back inside, wrapping a huge, fluffy white towel around her now-cold shoulders, that she noticed the answering machine blinking at her.

"It's so good to see you again," Gregory said, from across the cafe table. "I've missed you."

Claire smiled, repeating his words, but with an awed hush to her voice.

"Are you doing okay? You were kinda upset, you know, that day."

Seeing him again was strange, her mind kept flip-flopping between what her memories told her and what she'd come to love about the man whose hands had shaped those could-be vines, and might-be swans.

"I'm okay," she said. "I'm making do. The house is kind of empty, is all. But I'm doing all right. How are you doing? Still trying to scratch your name on heaven?"

His face seemed rounder, as if wherever he'd been had agreed with him. He looked less like the burning boy and more like a man recognizing a love of contentment. He had the same wild sways of brown hair, the same blue-green flecked eyes, but now his cheeks seemed less tight, his eyes less frantic.

He winced at her quote of his art philosophy, like a man being reminded that, as a boy, he used to wear sailor suits.

"Not as much. I'm working down at the University. It doesn't pay well, but I get all the supplies I need."

Claire smiled, remembering too many fights about money.

"You know," she said, "I miss your art. I've bought some but it isn't the same."

He smiled, showing teeth perhaps a little less white, a little more worn.

"I'm touched. I'm sorry I took everything."

"I've still got the fountain, of course. The one in the garden. You know, I've really learned to like it. I think it's your best work."

His frown aged him even more, but it was still too familiar from his many brooding nights.

"Oh, that."

He seemed to ponder something, staring down at the cafe table, his hands absently playing with a napkin.

"You know, it's funny, but that wasn't one of mine. I found it in this little junk shop and brought it home thinking I could do something with it. Just never did."

The waiter came, perfect timing, asking if they'd like coffee. Gregory said yes, as she shook her head in shock.

"Hey," he said, suddenly brightening, "I just remembered."

Reaching under the table, he produced a small portfolio case. Unsnapping it, he shuffled through sheets of thick sketch paper till he found what he was looking for.

"For you," he said with childish pride, "until, at least, I can do you something special."

The lines were crude, harsh and rough and insensitive. At first she thought it was a caricature, but then she realized that like all his art it was crude and meaningless.

She excused herself, lying that she had an appointment and lying that she'd call him.

* * * *

Dark clouds followed her home. As she put her key in the lock, the first drops tapped her, gently, on the top of her head.

By the time she kicked off her shoes and dropped her work clothes in a pile by the washer, the rain was pattering firmly on the roof and dancing in little geysers in the backyard.

Standing naked, looking at the fountain, she took two deep breaths before starting to walk, thinking: I've missed you.

DUST

Julie used to love the desert.

She used to see it as a place being born: unfinished, edges still rough, not yet smoothed by time and experience, full of raw, infant colors only beginning to wash out into taupes and pastels. She also used to see it as almost dead: full of bones and dusty rocks, spare of everything but the stubbornest forms of life. Either one she'd loved — completely, passionately.

That day, though, two steps behind her husband, she hated it.

The sun hammered her. It set fire to her hair. It blinded her eyes. Sweat trickled from a burning forehead. Her lips were cracked and broken.. Her sinuses whistled with every breath. The sun was alone in a featureless blue sky. Her clothes were simple and perfect for the time and place: white t-shirt, simple REI desert cap, tan shorts, good walking boots, and a day pack with more than enough supplies for a short hike in 90-plus-degree weather.

It wasn't how her body felt, because that's the way it always felt out in the hot, dry wastes of the desert. It was all part of the experience, an experience she used to love. No, it was because as she walked across the acid flats, she couldn't keep herself from thinking about the cool waters of the YMCA pool.

It was because of that, because of where her memory kept taking her, that she hated Stephen — and hated the desert she used to adore.

As she walked, she looked at the cracked lake bed, at the crazy-quilt of minuscule fissures and the curled, dried mud that crunched and crackled under her boots like dried leaves. She used to adore that sound and the fragility of the emptiness; this time, though, she found herself staring at Stephen's wide, strong back and with each step a fresh flare of anger.

A heavy wind swept over them, an invisible elephant of dry air, and Stephen made a mad grab for his hat it keep it from tumbling across the dead lake. Watching him, seeing the familiar play of muscles and the flash of his gentle, bearded face as he turned and clumsily caught his cap, it was all Julie could do to keep from running up to him and slapping his face.

But she didn't.

Instead, she just watched him catch his cap, wide smile beaming back at her.

"Almost," he said.

"Yeah," she said, trying to keep the venom out of her tones.

"Stop in a mile or so? That sound like a plan?"

"Yeah, that'd be fine."

Julie's legs throbbed. She blinked madly, trying to keep the sweat out of her burning her eyes. Finally reaching a point where she knew she had to, she brought her canteen to her lips and took a quick mouthful.

It was barely enough to unstick her tongue, but it was water, and with water came the memory of Rick — and the pool of the YMCA.

Swimming had seemed like a natural way to exercise. She'd done it before, in college, and then on and off afterwards. But after that stupid New Year's resolution (Stephen's idiotic idea) to exercise a bit more regularly, she'd been visited by a determination to do it every other night.

Besides, the Y was right down the street. A nice enough facility: clean, trainers on call, weight room, steam room, massage — and a nice big pool.

She shook her canteen, just once, to feel the water rattle in its stainless steel confines. Hiking through the sweltering heat of the desert, she closed her eyes and imagined there was a rolling sea in that bottle — imagined floating in it, lifted and suspended on cool water.

Besides, if she kept her eyes open she'd have to look at Stephen. She didn't want to do that.

She was a good swimmer, not great, but good. It didn't bother her at first, but after the second or third week her arms and legs had started to feel heavy, tense, packed with lead.

Rick, her swim trainer, was a lithe little man in his mid 30's. Not really handsome, she noted the first time she asked him for suggestions. His ears were like irregular outcroppings of cartilage on the side of his face and his nostrils were way too big, but he wasn't hard to look at. He was also handsome in certain ways. His shoulders were broad, like Stephen's, his chest well-defined, and his arms and hands like something Rodin might have chiseled out of marble.

She stumbled — as if the desert had decided it was being ignored so tripped her up to make her open her eyes, to make her acknowledge the stark emptiness they were trekking through. She used to appreciate it, see the flat expanse, the drifting sand, the glowing pastels and shimmering air, the too blue sky and painfully vast expanses.

And the nights? Who could forget a desert night: hard points of millions of stars shimmering down, casting faint shadows on the still-warm earth.

Stephen turned and smiled again — that innocent, almost childishly adoring smile that, once, had melted her heart. Now, he was a fool, an idiot. Seeing that smile, Julie fought an urge to scream at him. But before the impulse could peak he turned away, looking down the faint desert path.

She'd known what Rick had wanted the instant she'd started to talk to him — knew that he didn't care that she sported a small gold band on one hand. At first his attention, his lingering gaze and smile, had scared her. Then she began to look forward to her laps in the great pool and his merciless flirts.

That first time, he'd been holding her, supposedly helping her practice her kicks. His strong arms had been wrapped around her, bracing her against sinking in the harshly chlorinated water. She remembered scissoring her legs frantically, all the time too aware of his proximity and the way her body was responding.

When she'd gotten too tired, he'd helped her up; and then, arms still lingering around her waist, he'd kissed her. At first it had been a hard-lipped, chaste contact. Then suddenly she'd become as fluid as the water, melting into a hot dance of lips, tongue and mingled breaths.

They'd been the last swimmers of the day, so the pool had been deserted. She didn't know, and never really pondered, what might have happened if others had been paddling around the Olympic pool. She also never really pondered why she let the kiss go on, or why she didn't push him away when his hand went up to cup her breast, to rub a strong thumb across the tightness of her nipple.

Walking through the desert, she became even hotter. Knowing it was foolish, she uncapped her canteen and took another along long pull of tepid water. Ahead, Stephen stepped around a thick outcropping of weeds, tiny seeds suddenly appearing on his hairy legs. She wanted to scream, to shout at him, to punch him, to scratch him — anything to penetrate his cool ignorance of her shame.

Instead she just followed him, steps landing just short of his lengthening shadow.

That first night had been simple and almost adolescent: Rick's hand on her breast, his thumb stroking her nipple, his tongue moving her own; Rick's hand slipping under her strap, pulling it down. Julie's right breast, then her left, exposed to the cool water. She remembered the way a few gentle waves, the echoes of her kicking, had slapped against her belly, the way Rick's mouth found her right nipple, his tongue circling its crinkled peak. Rick's hand between her legs, gently massaging her.

Then, it was her hand on his strong shoulder. Her other hand, between his legs, tightly wrapped around his erection.

Details rolled through her mind as she walked: the biting smell of the chlorine, the bounding echoes of their heavy breathing off the great tiled expanse of the pool, the gritty bites of the rough concrete under her toes, the surges of cool water up against her body, the way she seemed to float, buoyed up by the pool … and by Rick's insistent erection.

They stopped at the top of a low desert rise. They didn't talk much on these long walks, and so her silence wasn't extraordinary.

He looked at her with his puppy-dog eyes: "How ya doin'?"

I fucked a trainer at the YMCA, she wanted to say. *He was hot, damned hot. We did it three times, every time in the water. I almost drowned giving him head.*

"I'm *fine*," she sneered, wiping her forehead with a handkerchief.

–and you're so stupid you can't even see it in my eyes–

* * * *

The desert is a thirsty place, endlessly craving any form of moisture: rain, sweat, even tears immediately soak up into the dry, dusty ground, vanish into the oven-hot air. But sometimes the desert doesn't like a hungry man looking at a feast and not eating, it savors water, enjoying the potential more than actually drinking.

The pool was tucked in behind a low rise, ringed with tufts of brown grass, like a secret the desert was trying to hide. The water was fairly clear, not okay to drink, but clean enough to wash in.

Looking down at the little pool, Julie had a flash of memory, occasional stillness of the Y's pool before she dove into it. Rare, as so many people jumped in so regularly, but it happened nonetheless, she used to consider it virginal water — before she'd taken Rick's cock in her mouth and mixed his saltiness with the bite of chlorine.

She never thought that water could make someone feel dirty. Now she knew differently.

Frowning into the still water, she bent down to dip her handkerchief — and was pushed in.

The murky surface rushed up at her, and in an instant she was in it and under it. Reaching out in panic, her hands plunged into thick, silty mud, and quickly pushed her head up into the air. Gagging from the gritty water she'd swallowed, she stood up in the center of the tiny pool, warm water cascading off her. The sound was discordant: a soaking shower in the middle of the baking desert.

Stephen was in hysterics. His face beamed in a delighted, maniacal grin.

His laughter cut through Julie like a razor. Furious, she rushed towards him, anger blurring her vision, shortening her breath. The tiny pond was congested with mud and algae though and instead of getting out she just tumbled back in again.

Hauling herself up, wiping the dirty water from her eyes, she was ready to scratch and claw him, furious at his prank — but, more honestly, his stupid, blind love for her. She'd done something awful, and he was too idiotic to notice it. A scream built in her throat, a hideous tension that wanted out — now! She was just about to let it, screech out the pain that was eating her guts when something splashed heavily down next to her, throwing her off balance again.

Stephen jumped into the pool. Windmilling her arms, Julie tried to regain her balance. The thick resistance of the water trapped her feet however and instead she toppled, this time backwards, into the pool and onto her ass.

With the blistering sun behind his head, his beard and long brown hair became a mad halo. Stephen looked, in that one second, like a figure out of time, a statue standing on a burning desert plain. It took her a moment to realize his hand was outstretched towards her.

She wanted to leap at him, to punch him with all her strength. She wanted to claw at him, to let the rage she felt out in screaming and tears.

His hand closed around hers before she realized what was going on. Vividly, she felt their wet palms slide against one another, the gritty water adding an interesting texture to the contact. He pulled, she tried to fight — but not that hard — and then they were standing together in the middle of a mineral spring, in the middle of the desert.

His lips found hers with a flavor of magnesium, a tang of sulfur, and a sliding, almost burning where their lips met. Without thought she opened her mouth to mix his hot breath with hers, an old, familiar ritual. His hands reached around to slip in and slide up her back under her t-shirt. The feeling made her feel warm, warmer than the furnace of the desert. They kissed for what felt like eons, longer than they ever had before. As they kissed, his hands went from her back, down to her hips, then back up and under again. Rough, strong, he then cupped her breasts, holding them. Not a lover's fondle, but rather just a safe, reassuring touch.

Their clothes were soaking, but they didn't move. In one quick gesture, her shirt and hat were off, tossed to the side of the pool. His hands returned to her breasts, her nipples rolled between his thumbs and forefingers. As always with Stephen, the feeling made her legs all but collapse under her.

Then, without a word, they sat in the middle of the tiny spring. Facing each other — the tepid water rolled against their chests, causing Julie's small breasts to bob and float among the bits of dried weed and brush floating on the surface — they kissed again.

She didn't need to check. She knew he was erect. It was a good, comforting knowledge.

As he stroked her shoulders, her cheek, her chest, her breasts she dropped a hand down to touch him. Gently stroking him through the thick, coarse canvas of his shorts, she relished in the bath water of the pool and the way it made her feel safe, protected.

Somehow they got their shorts off. The heavy, wet garments landed with matching plops on the pool's bank.

They'd made love in the water before.

A few times in rented hot tubs, even a few times at the beach. It was never a great experience, but something fun because of its uniqueness. But there, in that tiny pool, under the stern sun, it was good.

Slowly, cautiously, Julie moved onto his lap till his cock glided neatly between her legs. They rocked like that, not penetrating, but rather stroking each other with their bodies, for a long time.

It was shocking when they came, as if the goal hadn't been expected or even desired but was suddenly — bang! — there anyway.

Maybe because of their slow movements, their strangely controlled motions, or maybe because they both needed it so badly, their orgasms rocked quickly, almost quietly between them. It wasn't a screaming come, but rather a hissing, body-clenching kind of release — something deep, primordial, and special.

They rested, sitting in that warm desert pool for a long time.

Then, mutually, they realized it was getting late. Smiling, silent, they struggled into their clothes. It wasn't an easy task, and they both flashed childish grins at the irritating grit and sulfurous water that chafed and scratched as they struggled with their clothes.

Julie was the last to finish getting dressed. Standing in the pool, she methodically wrung out her handkerchief. Finally dry to her satisfaction, she started to plow forward through the murky water when she looked up and saw Stephen standing on the bank.

"Wait," he said.

Bending down, he scooped up a handful of the dirty water and, with surprising serenity, carefully poured it over her head.

As the water dribbled down her back, over her ears, and down almost into her eyes, Julie blinked, blinked, and blinked again — trying to stave off some of the tears that had started to gather. In the end she lost, and she sobbed. Her tears mixed with the pool's dirty water, vanishing.

Even dirty water can be cleansing — acknowledging, forgiving.

They marched through the hot, late afternoon to their car. Even though the heat still seemed to burn her face, Julie never let go of Stephen's hand.

GERTRUDE

He doesn't look like much. Still, when I look at the picture he sent me I get a quiet rush, a reverberation of what it was like.

I didn't feel anything like that when I knocked on his door that night, four years ago. It was routine, a noise complaint. I remember thinking, as I walked up the steps to the little house on 4467 Pierce Street, that anyone who blasted Beethoven couldn't be a lot of trouble to deal with. I was wrong.

He'd opened the door on the third knock. I sized him up the instant it swung open: white Caucasian male, 35 to 37 years old, approximately 140 pounds, curly brown hair, green eyes, no facial hair or obvious distinguishing markings. He'd been wearing jeans, tennis shoes, and a faded orange sweatshirt with the brooding face of his favorite composer whose *5th Symphony* was rattling the windows.

At the Academy they teach you never to make assumptions, that even the most innocent face can hide a nasty perp. "Treat every situation as a potentially dangerous one"– and if you do you'll freak out in a matter of months. It had taken me a while, more than anything because of who I am, my size, my age, that I'm a woman, but I'd still managed to develop a set of cop instincts. The Academy would say to watch your ass, but my guts said that he was just some innocent little music fan.

As it turned out, the Academy was closer to the truth.

"Shit!" he'd said, with a comic intensity that made me smile despite myself, "Sorry, Officer."

He dropped back into the place, moving quickly towards a wall-sized stereo set-up, and Beethoven dropped down to just a percussive rumble.

"Got a little carried away I guess. You know Ludwig. Gets your blood stirred up."

I can't remember what I said. I do remember, though, what I was staring at. You see a lot of shit when you're a cop, but in quiet little Bakersfield you don't see that much. I knew what I was looking at, of course. I'd seen more than my fair share in the magazines I kept hidden at home. Still, it was one thing to know something exists and quite another to see it personally.

I guess I must have stared for quite a while, because I was suddenly aware that he was looking at me. Shaking it off, I glanced at him and met a sly smile and those sparkling green eyes.

I didn't say a word as he closed the door behind me.

* * * *

My ID says GERTRUDE PARROW. I still hate Momma for that, a name no one — let alone a kid — should get stuck with. To everyone except the Sergeant it's Jeri — not Gerty, and certainly not Gertrude. Usually all it takes is a frown and a low growl to get it corrected.

The Academy taught me a lot of things that weren't on the curriculum. Like female officers will always get the shit work, especially in little burgs like Bakersfield, and that we're going to get damned little respect from citizens and especially from other cops. Momma always said I was a fast learner — and that was a lesson I picked up extra quick. After my first two weeks I put aside Gertrude and built up Jeri, a tightly-wound, non-nonsense, ball breaking bitch. Of course being a little over six foot helps, as does carrying 160 in firm muscles. Wasn't always that way, I had to build Jeri up in more ways than just attitude.

I was strong. I was mean. I was no one, even my 'fellow officers,' messed with. I was also lonely.

I attracted some men, of course, and even some women, but you could see in their eyes that they wanted Jeri and not the whole package, Jeri but also Gertrude.

Until that day he played Beethoven played too loud — and I saw the whip.

* * * *

I didn't ask "is it real?" as he got me a drink from the kitchen. I didn't need to — it had a very … lived-in look. Black leather strips, about a dozen or so strands. It looked heavy, it looked mean, it looked … I felt myself quietly go wet staring at it.

His name was — is — Julius. You wouldn't know it to look at him, old sweatshirt and running shoes, but he'd been doing this kind of thing for a while. Not obvious, but definitely there when he spoke:

"So, you want to play?"

It wasn't so much a question as a mocking observation. All I could do was nod as I sipped my drink.

"Then let's," he said, smiling broadly, eyes dancing. "Or would this be assaulting a police officer?"

I smiled back, reached up and plucked my badge from my shirt. Jeri was determined, Gertrude was hungry.

He started with a kiss — not a polite peck on the cheek, but rather a forceful, hot stab with his tongue. Grabbing the back of my very short ponytail he jerked me back, hard. Gasping for air, I instead would his firm, soft lips, and strong, passionate tongue. Down deep, I felt myself respond … on a very primal level.

"You're mine, slut," he said with a bass growl. "For the next hour you are mine — a possession, an object, a thing. You exist for one — and only one — thing: to pleasure me. Do you understand me, slut?"

I agreed. I tried to make it sound like "YESSIR!" but I'm afraid it was just little Gertrude by then, Jeri having stepped out with that first hard kiss, and instead it came out "yes … sir …."

"Now strip — show me what you've got," he said, pulling up a battered chair and sitting, facing me.

Those men, and those few women, they'd wanted me to say those words, to growl commands, orders — but all that time I wanted to hear them, too — to put aside the badge, gun, the attitude .. to put aside Jeri.

I stood, slowly because my knees were weak, and started to unbutton my shirt. I didn't intend to do it slowly, but my fingers were shaking. One button, two, three. Shirt off. Then my boots, comically hopping braced against a doorjamb — but he didn't laugh. No, he watched. Not stared, just watched, with a gleam in those green eyes like a falcon or a leopard. I didn't know if he was going to fuck me … or consume me — and that made me all the wetter.

Naked, I stood in front of him, my juices painting my inner thighs with a sheen of want. He smiled, cruelly, and stood. He inspected me, looking at my heavy tits, my crinkled nipples, my ass, my belly, my neck, my face, into my eyes.

"You'll do," he said after a while.

"Thank you, Sir," I said in a weak voice, the carpet swaying beneath my feet.

"As an object you must meet my needs, satisfy my every desire. Do you understand me, slut?"

"Yes, Sir," I said, distinctly aware of my throbbing clit, the ache in my nipples.

Then he said it, and if I was flowing before I practically streamed after.

"Suck my cock," he said, a growl in his words, steel in his tones.

He was impressive, but I'd seen larger. But it wasn't just his cock I was begging for. He was hard, a thick length of cock sticking out of his pants, and that got me even wetter, not for the sight of it but rather the command, the order.

I got down on my knees and started to suck him like his was the only cock in the world.

Done others, probably will do many others, but his was my Master's cock, the cock I'd been ordered to suck, and so nothing could compare to it. Single-mindedly, becoming just an ecstatic sucking machine, I worked on him — his slight moans and groans a glorious kind of applause for my technique. I wanted more than anything to please him.

I guess I got a little too enthusiastic. The joy at being pushed down, at being released from my bounds as the dominant Jeri, was a little too much for him. His small yelp was like glass shattering, as if a part of my ideal world. The world of Gertrude the sucking slave broke, fell apart.

"Bad," he said, pulling his cock out of my mouth and sticking it back into his pants, "very bad. Obviously you're in need of some training, because a real slave, an ideal slut, would never, ever, allow her teeth to even graze the cock of her Master."

Jeri was frightened of nothing, but Gertrude — little slutty Gertrude — was terrified.

"I'm so sorry, Sir –" I pleaded in a soft voice, bowing towards his simple running shoes. "Please, I didn't mean to –"

I couldn't see his face, but I could hear the sneer in his voice.

"Begging is so pathetic — even for a slut. Obviously you're in need of some *severe* discipline."

That was it. Right then I knew what was coming next. The magazines I'd bought with their lurid fleshtones and shocking titles had prepared me some, but not enough. They'd shown me the position, on my hands and knees, head down on the old carpeting, ass high in the air, legs slightly spread to bare the lips of my cunt. But they never, and never could have, gotten me ready for the first impact of the whip.

I expected pain, but it was more than that. At first it was a gentle slap, a glancing blow across both my cheeks. That's it? I remember thinking, almost frowning into the carpet, but then there came the next blow — harder, faster — and I knew that wasn't it. Oh, no, that wasn't it at all –

The impacts came faster, a pounding rhythm that may have started on my ass but soon became a drumming tremor through my whole body. It was as if my entire being was being beaten with a regular 4x4 beat, a drum in his sensual, masterful concerto.

My ass warmed, becoming almost hot, and my cunt felt molten, melting further with each thud of the whip. Each beat was like a great wave rolling through my body, starting at my cunt and rippling through my belly, into my deep guts, thrilling my nipples and then out my mouth. At first I thought the sound was from somewhere else. It wasn't until later that I realized that I'd groaned with each impact, an echoing deep rumble to his regular beating.

Jeri was nowhere to be found. It was just the slut, Gertrude, receiving her exquisite punishment, and it was wonderful.

He said something, and it stopped, the cessation as shocking as the first impact. Distantly, I was aware that he reached down and helped me up, led me like a sleepy child deeper into his apartment.

After, I looked closer at the room — noticed the great bookshelf of dusty, and dog-headed volumes, the rack of CD's, the small pile of dirty laundry … and the brass bed. But as he led me in, I didn't see anything but his hard hand gripping my wrists, then the bed itself, vast and comforting.

"You have pleased me, slut," he said, as if from a long distance. "You have pleased me with your performance, but there's one last thing I require."

I knew what was coming next, as if a deep part of Gertrude was following some passionate script. Again, my face was down, this time in a soft comforter, arms outstretched to grip the cool metal of the brass bed. Again, my legs apart, my ass high, but this time not to receive the whip.

He entered me, cock sliding effortlessly into my hot cunt. He fucked me, and again, like with the whipping, time vanished and I became his object, his slut. I lived for his pleasure, existed to service him.

It was wonderful.

We fucked that first time for what felt like hours, his strokes rocketing through me as the whip had, but this time the impacts echoed through my body, not just from my reddened ass. Slowly, he pushed me higher and higher, quickly up a slope I'd only climbed before with one of my forbidden magazines and a vibrator.

Then it happened, and shortly thereafter for him as well. The ecstasy was like a brilliant light in my eyes, a body rush, and a dreamlike collapse onto the soft comforter, onto his brass bed.

That was the first. There were many times after. Officer Jeri may have knocked on his door that first time, but it was slutty little Gertrude who returned time and time again.

Fires die, people change. Eventually it faded for both of us. There have been others since, more Masters and even some Mistresses, but he'll always remain special, a first step on a long and wonderful road.

Every once and a while, I still take his photo out of my wallet and stare at his face, at those stern green eyes, and Gertrude smiles.

DEAD LETTER

"What does ectoplasm taste like?" said a woman in a floral print sundress, hand quivering in the air. Her eyes gleamed with enthusiasm, the asking more important than the answer.

"An interesting question," he said, coughing into his hand for dramatic effect. "One I'm very glad you've asked. Even though most parapsychologists have discovered that what we call 'ectoplasm' is actually just common atmospheric debris: dust, pollen, fibers from clothing, skin flakes, and so forth suspended in moisture drawn out of the air. In my own experiments, the few times I've ingested the material, usually in a spectral erotic activity mirroring a common sexual practice where body fluids would normally be sampled, I've found the taste to be much closer to that of a real woman than the contents of a dustpan."

The audience laughed, hearty and honest, a few claps of hesitant applause popping in the middle. The woman, pleased by his, and the rest of the crowd's response, grinned widely and sat down.

"I've actually given quite a bit of thought to these rare occurrences where I've been able to experience 'taste' during a visit, as well as other similar instances where she has appeared to have a much more 'real' substance than usual during one of her appearances in this, our domain. Many times, for instance, I've had the experience of a visitation feel much more … substantive, I guess you could say, than I'd ever think a ghost could be. It is my belief that these visitations are unique because my visitor and I have been able to establish a much more direct joining, a direct spiritual connection between myself and my other-worldly partner."

He's certainly on a roll, Juliet thought, bored and stiff, cautiously stretching out a stocking foot, twisting, turning it, hoping no one noticed.

The next came from a scraggly student-type, stringy hair ponytailed, face clearly not intimate with a razor.

"Hi — uh — I'm Eric. I have a question about the potion you said you use in *Sleeping With the Dead*. Can you, like, say what it is? So other people can, like, do this stuff, too?"

Randolph grinned, the white thicket of his beard rising at the corners of his almost-invisible mouth.

"Sorry to disappoint but the elixir that I use to put me into the right vibrational state to receive my other-worldly visitations was specially formulated for me by a High-Born Guru of Kaderistan, who gave it to me during one of my adventures in that far away land. Before he gave it to me, he made he swear on my Immortal Soul never to allow another to use it, for the gates between the realms are as fragile as they are powerful and the risks for the uninitiated to cause damage to both the earthly as well as the ethereal domain is far too great."

Oh, yeah, Kaderistan — a real vacation spot. While you were out getting 'enlightened' I was squatting over a hole in the floor crapping my guts out, she thought, hiding a yawn behind the back of a hand.

"Bummer..." the scraggly young man mumbled, falling back into his seat.

"Any more questions?" Randolph asked, scanning the bookstore with his sincerely blue eyes. "I'm very pleased to see such a large turn-out. Always wonderful to know that my message of sensual relations with the dead has managed to reach so many people."

At twenty bucks a pop for paperback, and ten percent to us, I'm damned happy about it too. Looking over the crowd she didn't see any more hands. *Great. maybe we'll be able to get out of here after only the usual hour of autographs.*

"I have a question."

She was young, pretty, toned as only someone to whom sag was only a word could be.

"Certainly, dear," Randolph said, the beard twitching. "Ask me anything."

"How does your wife feel about this? I mean, having sex with ghosts –" the girl glanced at Juliet, stance and lifted chin a challenge to step up to the feminist bat and be struck out.

"My wife and I have a very special relationship," he said, gesturing to where Juliet sat. "She is very understanding towards my mission to reach the spectral realm with my erotic energies and so try and understand the nature of the afterlife. I could not pursue this great mission, and write the books you all seem to enjoy, without her help."

Very special is right, Juliet thought, hoping the sneer didn't peer around the corners of her stage smile.

* * * *

"What a very pleasant evening," he said as they walked in the door, coats going on hooks. "So exciting to see others as excited as I am about erotic contact with the other world."

"That's definitely what I'd call it: 'exciting.' That's the word I'd use," she said, dropping her keys in a Tibetan prayer bowl. *Definitely.*

"I believe that was one of the largest audiences I've ever had. Don't you think so, beloved?"

Math in her head, autographs and book sales. She smiled.

"Why, I do believe it was."

"I can only hope the next book will do as well. Dare I hope it will be even more successful?"

Oh, dare — dare! For our bank account — dare!

"No reason to think it won't be. Each one's sold better than the last."

"Oh, Juliet, how you inspire me! You are truly a wonderful and enlightened being to support me in my spiritual journey."

Smiling firmly, she took his hand from her shoulder.

"Well, Randolph, you inspire me as well. We're a team, right?"

"How correct you are, beloved. How correct you are," he beamed. "Oh, I can hardly wait to make my next contact with the Great Beyond! Meeting those people who so believe in my work has tremendously energized me."

'Energized,' oh great. "That's wonderful. It's always wonderful when you're excited about your work."

"Do you think it's too early to make an expedition, beloved? I know I can be severely... well, I guess you could say depleted after such a transport and would hate to abandon you for the evening."

"Thanks for your concern, Randolph, but don't worry about me. Are you up for it? Don't want to burn yourself out, you know. Nothing wrong with taking a rest, putting your feet up and all. You don't have to travel every time you lie down, you know."

"Ah, but the spirits are all but begging me to see them tonight. Can't you feel them? I can. Tonight they're particularly eager for me to visit them, to engage in our ... um, eh, ah, contact. They do not get much contact with the flesh, you know."

Lucky stiffs.

"I understand, darling. I really do. I'm just saying that maybe you just want to rest up rather than working. We both... I mean, you had a very busy day."

"Who do you think will come tonight, beloved? Perhaps Maybe Marie Antoinette? Marilyn? Or what about Cleopatra? It seems like ages since she crossed over. She might be just about due."

Oh, no — not her. Too much work. "Like I said, don't get your hopes up too much. After all, there'll always be other nights."

"But I can feel them, Julia. All around me, just waiting for a chance, as do I, to join in communion between the spheres, to join in spectral rapport! Besides, think of the books. Think of all those people, like the ones we met tonight, who are so eagerly awaiting my next volume of spiritual traveling. For them I shall Walk the Road Between the Worlds, explore the sensual and erotic domains between the living and the expired!"

Oh, Lordy. "Well, I can see that you're very ... excited right now, Randolph. It might be better to relax and not push the spirits, if you know what I mean. Maybe they need a night off, just like you."

"Oh, my beloved Juliet, you are such a caring and devoted spouse. Your concern for me is so tender and caring, but I assure you I'm hearty and healthy if not even more so than usual. Tonight has been rejuvenating! Meeting all those eager readers, the books doing so well, and especially with your loving support. It's all so wonderful!"

Was she blushing?

"Oh, knock it off, Randolph –"

"And I owe it all to erotic contact with ghosts! Who would have thought of it?"

Yeah, right, ghosts — who would have thought...

"Well, if you are going to travel to the Other World, shouldn't you be getting to bed, dear?"

* * * *

Helen of Troy — diaphanous, luminous, ethereal — glided into the room, and banged her shin on the coffee table.

Dammit! she thought, biting her lip so as not to put speech to it. Hopping, balancing with a hand tightly around an ornately carved bedpost, she vigorously rubbed her barked ankle.

"W-what–?" came Randolph's sluggish voice from a point somewhere below a mountain range of goose down pillows.

Crap! Both feet down, ankle clearly more painful than damaged, she smoothed her sheet, adjusted her dimestore tiara, took a deep breath and crooned out a melodious "*Oooooooooooooo!*"

Then, whispering down low near her husband's ear: "From the great beyond, I have come!"

"W-who is there? Who is it?"

The lights in the room were dim, so much so that everything seemed washed with a brush dipped in inky shade and shadow. The bed was a pale rectangle, the pile of pillows a gray smudge, her husband's face a pale mask haloed by silver hair — and that damned coffee table completely invisible.

"Men launched a thousand ships for me," she softly crooned, exhausting her knowledge of the character.

"I-I h-heard that was … mythology," Randolph mumbled, head rolling gently back and forth, words leaden from his meditative tincture.

Crap, she mentally repeated, hoping to remember to do more research.

"Oh, the wonders of the flesh," she said, skipping her fingers down his nightgown-covered chest.

Growling, a tiger rumble of excitement, he rolled and stretched sensually. Legs mirroring, moving lethargically under the sheets, his hands floated up, clearly trying to find her. Clumsy and unfocused, they never came close.

"How I've missed this."

She completely pulled back the sheet, which had already been turned down. Stretched out, her husband's body gently undulated in the murky light, his dressing gown pearly white. Here we go again.

"W-welcome b-back," he whispered, a hand finally finding her shoulder, sliding down — then off — her arm.

"Returning is so … satisfying," she murmured, fingers continuing to trip down his chest. Not for the first time she was gently distracted by how tight his chest was. Not a young man he was still remarkably toned, she stroked down muscles over skin that was only just starting to show the other side of middle age.

"T-thanks for c-coming."

A smile curled the corners of his mouth, making his face all of a sudden delightfully radiant.

Hand further down, she suddenly made contact with something remarkably harder. *Oh, my* — while not rare for him to be excited by her ghostly nocturnal visitations, tonight he was remarkably aroused. The erection she brushed was tight and hard, and raised at a very determined angle. Without a thought she wrapped her hand around it, relishing its strength.

"My … pleasure," she said, perhaps a bit too loudly as she began to gently stroke him through the fabric of his gown.

Ecstatic, he undulated on the bed, bottom sheet tugging almost free from the corners, but cock staying firmly in her hand.

Normally — and she grinned, curling the corners of her own mouth at that for it seemed like nothing about their lives was anything close — it would be a simple, direct night, just enough to fuel his delusion. Delusion + books = money, after all. But right then, cock in her hand, she didn't want to coolly stroke it until he came, a nocturnal (spiritual) emission on the sheets.

Gown up, eyes adjusted to the low light, she could see what she'd been feeling. Many had called Randolph handsome, especially when he was younger, but she'd never really agreed. Pleasant to look at, easy on the eyes, striking in his own way perhaps, but not really handsome, per se. But now as she assessed his cock, she had to finally nod her head and join that crowd at least for that one part of him, that night.

A nice cock, a fine erection. It felt good in her hand: strong and eager, emerging from a curly thicket of gray and black hairs, dark walnuts barely visible lower, at the junction of his slightly parted legs.

At the tip, at tiny cleft, a pearl gleamed in the soft darkness, set in the smooth, plump head a drop of early excitement, promise of orgasm.

Then, before she was conscious of it, something else — tasty. Her head was down, lips parted and he was inside her mouth. Initially she simply relished the way the size and firmness of him filled her, the way the plump, swollen corona rested against the roof of her mouth, against her tongue. Then she wanted more. Same tongue, same mouth, same lips, she began to really feel and taste the cock inside her. Rolling and flicking all over (tongue), smooth against rough palate (mouth), soft glide down and up the shaft (lips), she closed her eyes, moaned a bit, and drifted away into the pleasure of sucking him.

The pleasure was clearly mutual. Senses distorted but also amplified, he groaned deep and primeval, arms and legs sweeping back and forth (arms) and open, closed (legs) as she rolled her lips, tongue and mouth up and down his cock. In the midst of his deep sounds a few words bubbled up.

"Oh, m-my ...." being the most clear and articulate.

What in the hell am I doing? But while it was certainly articulate the answer wasn't clear, though it should have been, considering the formula of delusion + scorn = frustration. Getting on the bed, clumsy in her eagerness, she kept her one hand on him while she fought with the tangled wrap of her muslin toga. Under was nothing but skin and between her legs, she absolutely knew, she was slick and wet and very hot.

One leg on one side, other on the other, she stroked him, tipping the head of his erection across her own tangle of black and white curls, slicking between her lips with delightful restraint.

"Oh … oh," came his fuzzy voice, his aimless words from near that range of goose down. Still fluttering, ill-controlled, his hands still managed to land again on her shoulders, but this time they slipped along her arm down to her breasts. There, they feverishly caressed them, clumsily pushing aside muslin to expose plumpness and the aroused hardness of her dark brown nipples.

"Beautiful," he slurred, eyes dancing, sparkling with unfocused but obviously wild excitement as his hands roamed her body.

"So … beautiful," he repeated, actions earnestly continuing.

Above, still feeling his excitement between her lips, she felt her temperature hit the top of her thermometer. Blushing hotly, she pushed him back, head of his cock slipping then hovering just below where she wanted him. Then, dropping herself down, she was there, inside.

Inside.

And she sighed, her voice thunderous in the barely lighted, hushed room. Pausing for just a moment, she let her desire drive her up and down on his hardness, own vision blurring, own mind fogged. Up and down, up and down, hips rocking, rising and falling to push herself down, forcing him in deeper.

Below her, his body convulsed, tightened, relaxed, tightened, relaxed with her up and down thrusts and giggling squirms. Gasping, moaning, his hands nevertheless kept kneading at her breasts, tugging just right at her nipples. Eyes rolling, head flopping back and forth, "oh … oh …." from his tightened lips.

She felt it, novelty of its cause only heightening its arrival. Muscles gripped, back tensed, mouth wide, her moans climbed to a near scream.

Joining her in release, in rolling, pounding orgasm, his eyes were wide in wondrous, delighted comprehension, his body locked right in rigid muscles. No scream, though.

Instead a word, then another, then that special, last one: "Thank … you … Juliet."

Then it was there, and their bodies moved one last time, their voices chorused in pleasurable sounds until quiet, until relaxation, until exhaustion and she collapsed down, face on his cool chest, though still panting with echoes of body joy tickling her between her legs, at the tips of her nipples.

After a minute, maybe two or even three: "Randolph … oh, Randolph, that was wonderful." Tears, hot on her cheek. "I've missed that. I've really missed that."

After four, perhaps three or even four: "I'm so sorry, dear. I hated lying all this time but … you seemed so excited, so happy. I hadn't seen you like that in a long time. Then when the books began to do so well, I just … I just began to resent it, I guess. See you for a fool. But you're not, you're really not — and I'm … I really am sorry."

But then, after ten, even eleven minutes, her voice shocked and high: "Randolph? Randolph!"

* * * *

"What does ectoplasm feel like?" said a pudgy little man in a t-shirt proclaiming that FRODO LIVES! His eyes were full of suspicion, his question no doubt lying in some sort of trap.

"Well, it doesn't feel like anything I've ever felt before. I don't know the science of it, but I always think it's something like smoke. You know you really can't 'feel' smoke, just that sometimes it's hot. I think ghost stuff is like that. You can't feel it, not really, but there's something in it you can feel like the hotness of a ghost. I hope that helps."

Disarmed, he looked embarrassed, he sat down, making his shirt's statement illegible over his rolling belly.

"Any other questions?" the bookstore owner said, a perky and bright bird of a woman, clearly delighted in the turn-out.

A prim woman, stiff and armored in a tweed suit.

"I know what you say in your book, but I'd love to hear again about your feelings for your late husband."

The question seemed tinged with choked-up romance, the possibility of happiness even if it had to come after death.

Sitting in the front row, in a seat she'd specially reserved just for him, Randolph looked up at her and smiled. Through his wavering transparency she could see that the prim woman had ugly patent leather shoes.

"Even after his transportation to the other side, my husband and I have never been closer," Juliet said, returning her husband's sweet smile. "Randolph and I maintain a very special, and very loving, relationship."

THE TRAIN THEY CALL THE CITY OF NEW ORLEANS

The rails were clicking and clacking out a message. Maggie was sure, but it was one she didn't want deciphered or explained. She knew the nature of it, after all, if not the exact words: *Come back.*

A seductive message, an alluring bait hidden in the sounds of the train, but she'd escaped. She'd made it to the station, boarded the 6:15 to Atlanta, and she wasn't coming back.

The train rocked her gently over uneven rails, a slow side-to-side sway that reminded Maggie of being on a ship caught in low swells. Closing her eyes, she pictured herself sailing somewhere: the ocean patiently rolling around her, the warm wooden deck under her bare feet. It was a thin illusion. She'd never been on the ocean, but it was better than thinking of where she had been.

She tried to put herself on that ship or boat, whatever, anywhere but back in that hot city. The tiny overhead air conditioning jet became a cool breeze coming off the waves.

Thin, perhaps, but Maggie suddenly had a surge of nausea. Smiling ironically at her suddenly too-successful illusion, she opened her eyes. A threadbare Amtrak coach: a scattering of tired travelers, the backs of their heads poking above their seats, a wide-ranging display of beehive hairdos and male pattern baldness; the gray distance blurring by the darkly tinted windows.

Turning, she watched the streaking view, her eyes catching on sudden details, barely registering before the train's heavy momentum rushed it away: the green blur of close trees, the distant stroll of far ones, the scintillating snake of a side road, the sudden flash of crossings, the diagonal rush of a steel bridge. That last one, the bridge, brought a surge of fear. Maybe that bridge was the long one again, the one that had started her journey. But all the bridges remained short, and her anxiety flickered away. The Mississippi was behind her, as was the city on its shore, and its delta.

So much left behind: six months of paintings, some clothes, some cheap furniture, a photo or two. Some of it, she knew, she'd miss, but not for long, not after remembering why she'd escaped.

Evil city, she thought, *a bad place.*

It had done things to her. The hot days, the hot nights, the slow, sensual lethargy, the undulating accent, the peppery meals, it had all seeped into her. It mixed with her normally cool, reserved, immaculate body and will. There, she'd steamed in the heat, had burned with a slow fire.

It had frightened her. She'd grown up in the high latitudes, the cold and rainy pine forests of Oregon's Pacific Northwest. The days there had been thick with fog, the nights drowning in freeing rain. The only thing hot had been the bitter coffee.

Her early works had been local, her home town flowing from her brushes onto the canvas: gray, black, white, and a deep, impenetrable green. She'd painted vistas and views, sky and landscapes. Like her works, Maggie had surrounded herself with the same colors, the same views. The world, while she was there, had been glacial and patient.

Light. It had been so totally missing in that overcast town that she had even been alien to the idea, then a chance visit to a museum. Brilliant, warm, burning, blinding, she'd stood before the reds and yellows for what felt like years, but what were probably just minutes. A month later she was packed in her tired little Volvo and was on the road in search of the place where such shades lived, wild and free.

It had taken some time in the new city, but eventually the colors of New Orleans had started to work their way into her, seeping from the oil on her brushes and pallet through her skin and then down deep. Subtle, for such brilliance, almost unnoticeable.

Someone bumped into her elbow, jogging her memory. With a sharp shock, she straightened.

"Sorry," said a heavy voice from above.

His smile was bright, beaming as it was tossed back at her from over his right shoulder. Her artist's eyes picked him apart: the dull reds of his wool shirt, the aqua and white of his worn jeans, the terra-cotta of his comfortable leather boots, the marbling of his black and white peppered curly hair and beard. The smile stayed a bit too long, a touch stretched out as he took a seat three rows ahead of her.

That damned place, she thought, *that awful place.*

Iron balconies and brick, a turgid river moving with eternal purpose, shanty-shacks and mansions, crawfish and red peppers, too-sweet drinks and strong shots, an atmosphere of vomit and magnolia blossoms. She'd begun there as if it was just the same as the Pacific Northwest, just warmer, with more colors.

But then, it had started. Slowly, as said, insidious. Laying awake on a hot night, fanning herself with a magazine, body bare for a simple cotton dress. Thoughts had emerged, and she'd found herself pacing, at first in her mind and then with her feet, like a trapped jungle cat.

She'd had lovers before, of course, but they'd been intellectual, artistic interludes, executed with caution. They had either faded away, leaving nothing but memories, or had broken apart with only a few tears. But after she'd started renting that little place, the high-ceilinged loft near the river, she'd begun to crave, to hunger, in a way that was unfamiliar. Maggie had eaten before, but now she wanted to hunt and feast.

On the train, leaving that hot and humid city, she looked at the back of his head, recapturing for herself the breath of his shoulders, the tightness of his stride, the strength of his legs, the firm muscles of his back and ass. It was too easy to picture him, standing on the rough boards of her studio floor, clothes piled into a far corner. Standing firm and large, before her. She saw her hands as holding a bit of charcoal, capturing the flow of him, the planes and curves of his broad, firm body on a sketchpad.

It had been that place. It had hexed her, seeped into her open pores, worked its way into her. All that light, heat, spices, had done something to her. It had started burning her, making her smoke and steam.

She started masturbating. Casually at first, but then with a passion for herself that no lover had ever shown. It became an act of love, a thought-out and anticipated event. She'd spend the sweltering days thinking of a fantasy, constructing in her vivid imagination the location, feel, the color of his eyes, the sound of his voice, the words he'd speak, the feelings that would come to her.

She'd sketch him, capturing him on a few scraps of paper: his face, his chest, his arms, his legs, his penis — both hard and soft. Then, prepared and burning even hotter as the sun set on the filigreed rooftops, she'd stretch out on her cheap little bed, pull up her simple cotton dress, and tangle her fingers, at first, in the curls of her pubic hairs, and then with a few deft strokes part her lips and relish in the humid excitement of her cunt. Her other hand would be reserved for her tight nipples, the right when she wanted the familiarity of her favorite breast, the left for when she imagined his mouth, hand, there. It would go on for hours, and then even longer as the reds and yellows of her pallet, of the city, had started to really penetrate her skin.

On the train, leaving at last, she felt the heat again. The heavy, hot glow started in her lap and spread up her chest, forming twin flares of warmth at the tips of her breasts. Looking at the back of his head, she conjured him more fully. The curls of his peppered beard, the wrinkles around his nose, the fullness of his lips. She closed her eyes briefly and sketched in her mind the charcoal outlines of his strong legs, the flat muscles of his chest and belly, the unashamed determination of his hard cock. Focusing, feeling the reds and yellows of that far-off city, she even conjured for her imagination the pearly tip of early excitement swelling at the tip and the silken embrace of her lips descending and tasting its sharp saltiness.

She was too hot. In the cool cabin of the 6:15 to Atlanta, she was molten. It was familiar, as typical as any day she'd spent in New Orleans like the now-distant city had somehow stoked up the embers she'd thought she'd cooled by stepping onto the train.

Looking out the window again, Maggie tried to bring back the cool patience that'd insulated her, before the heat, before the reds and yellows, before the sweltering Summers, before the warm winters, before New Orleans, but it was like trying to speak a language long out of practice.

The blurring trees didn't bring it back, and neither did the quick flashes of power and phone poles. Instead, she thought about Louis. Tall, thin Louis, with the eyes like ball bearings. Young Louis, maybe just in college. They didn't talk about such things together. In fact they rarely spoke at all. Louis had come into her life one very hot summer day, a burnish, ebony young man who had helped deliver a crate of paints and books she'd had shipped from Seattle. He'd stayed, fascinated by the images captured on her canvases, then he stayed even longer after Maggie had allowed her hands to play along the strength of his back and shoulders.

She'd had lovers, yes, but none who burned like Louis, who smoldered and smoked like that young man. She hadn't done it out of curiosity, or as a way of getting to closer to something she'd wanted. No, Louis *had been* what she wanted, he was a blistering conflagration.

The view didn't cool the fire, and certainly recalling the passion of young Louis didn't. The fire was roaring now, a steaming kind of blaze that made her body a hothouse, a sauna. Her nipples ached from the heat, and from the absence of lips and hands on them. Her legs throbbed and quivered, like she'd been sitting for too long.

Finally, just a second before she thought she'd start to smoke, she got up. The action of her breasts changing position sent a quiver of body rush through her. She worked her way forward along the cabin. As she passed the man, the salt and peppered man, she actually tilted herself to one side to brush a strong hip against his shoulder.

"Excuse me," Maggie said in a harsh whisper, stretching the words like a curled finger towards him.

Seeing herself smile at him — a lingering, hungry smile — she almost rushed, almost ran to the bathroom.

The city had done it to her, surrounded her with steam and skin, with stretched syllables and spices. It had seduced her with its lazy sensuality, the kind that turned not-lazy but ferocious when the heat clicked from 90 to 91. It had turned Maggie from fog and pine needles into a woman with hot skin, tight nipples, a molten cunt. It had brought her a young man with driving hips, a long cock, and firm lips. The city had done it.

In the bathroom, the flames licked up between her legs. She wanted Louis with her now, wanted his slightly frightened smile as she took her dress off before him, wanted his handsome cock and too-tight ass. She wanted the peppered man from five or six rows back there, wanted his own long, proud cock, thick and strong, wanted his broad chest and tight muscles under her hands, wanted his hard little nipples in her mouth.

Dress up, clumsy in the tiny room, humid panties rushed to her thighs, then her ankles when she realized that she couldn't spread her legs far enough. She touched herself.

Fingers down. She wasn't wet, 'wet' wasn't the right word. It was as if she was steam itself her fingers met moisture but mostly heat, like putting her fingers in a cup of too-hot coffee laced with chicory.

It didn't take long. That was the exaltation, that was the explosive. No long fingering, no long fuck, no minutes and minutes of kissing and licking. One, two, three fingers down between her slick, hot, thighs and up into herself: slippery lips, humid moisture, pearly-hard clit, and the explosion, the burst up from down between her legs and up into her brain, her mind.

She screamed. She was sure of it, but didn't care … at the time.

∗ ∗ ∗ ∗

Shame followed her from the bathroom, down the aisle, and to her seat. She was hot, but not the humid excitement that had started in the city. No, it was a flushed humiliation, a sunburn of disgrace.

She hated that city. Hated what it had done to her, made her into. She wasn't Maggie the painter anymore. She wasn't calm and contemplative.

83

She was Maggie the hungry cunt, Maggie the sweating girl with hungry mouths.

She hated New Orleans — and hated what it had turned her into.

Looking out the window, she felt the tears, the burning acid of salt on her cheeks. When would it ever leave her alone, when would its drumming magic leave her alone? It was as if the streets, balconies, lilting accents had entangled with her, trapped her.

She looked out the window and cried for herself, cried from shame and fear, control completely gone, washed away by the stone streets and the great, lethargic Mississippi. She looked, and cried... the green streaks of hills, the strobes of fences and power lines, the distant stroll of much-more-distant hills and stands of trees.

Then she saw it, and the tears stopped their slow crawl down her cheeks. She saw those same iron balconies, those same smiling faces, those same cobbled streets, that same great river. It was there, in front of her, reflected in the window.

Then and there she knew she could never escape; it had been foolish to try.

* * * *

The station was quiet, the night late and cold. The absence of heat felt strange, goose pimples being something that felt so much better when it was excitement, and not absence of warmth. But she tolerated it, endured it, waiting with a glow of anticipation for the next train.

She couldn't wait to get back. It was where she belonged.

She knew it, staring out that window, knew that the city would follow her everywhere. She knew, seeing her reflection in the glass, that New Orleans would be every street, every building, every face in the crowd because the heat of that city wasn't on the shore of the Mississippi at all.

Standing on the platform, waiting for the flashing light of an engine, she held herself and smiled for the first time in many weeks, a deep, knowledgeable smile. New Orleans was her home, she knew, because it would always be inside herself. She couldn't ever leave it, escape it, because it was herself — the fires hers, the warmth hers, the passion hers, just as she'd seen her face reflected in that window.

Cold — but knowing soon, very soon, that she'd be warm again — she waited for the train to take her back to her home, and the special person she'd become there.

THE WILL OF DR. MABUSE

Professor Baum knew Nurse Harbou was standing next to him, a specter in starched white, but he didn't turn his head, even as she spoke.

"Any change, Professor?"

The silent door within the Berlin Psychiatric Institute was made of heavy, banded iron. The walls up and down the corridor still, solid stone vanished into high vaults, fogged with cobwebs. Beyond the door's narrow observation slot, room five was quiet, dipped in twilight from the single high, thickly barred window. The patient in room five hadn't moved from where he stood, staring at the Professor with cold and calculating eyes.

Professor Baum didn't respond to the nurse. He didn't wish to. Turning his head to look at her would inspire thoughts of undergarments, dappled sunlight on pale skin, hot breath. His pathetic infatuation with Nurse Harbou was a source of much shame, but somehow to feel it while standing there in the hallway, in front of the man in room five, made it worse. Professor Baum knew no God, had rarely stepped foot in any church, but he knew that if he did turn his head to behold the femininity of the nurse, it would somehow conjure within him a sense of impropriety.

Her hand was on his shoulder, a weight that sent a panicked lightness up through his being. Words not spoken but meaning nonetheless concern for his silence. The animal in him responded with redness that rose to his cheeks. He hadn't turned, hadn't looked at her, yet he still felt the heat from such a childish infatuation.

As if in response to his weakness, Dr. Mabuse, the man in room five, stepped into the growing shadows, vanishing into the darkness of his cell.

★ ★ ★ ★

85

The file of Dr. Mabuse consisted of merely words scratched onto vellum, typed onto foolscap, neatly itemized and categorized. Birth records, school records, police records, newspaper accounts. Papers, though, did not make a man. In fact, the papers simply seemed to swirl around the man in question, defying his being by what they didn't say, like the dark core of a cyclone.

The newspaper documents held the most fascination for Professor Baum. The records and reports spoke his language and he could see their glaring errors, knew all their legalized lies because he too had used the same phrases and terms. But the clippings and carefully typed transcriptions of radio broadcasts were another matter. Reading them, he felt himself become like a child, listening to tales of a mythical monster rampaging through all of Germany.

'Genius' was one of the words used in the reports and files from the Ministry of Police. But that only categorized the threat. It didn't describe the art. Like a silent conductor, Mabuse stood before the stock exchange, through his agents and power of will taking it from boom to bust in a few minutes. Across all of Berlin, Mabuse ruled the underworld, terrifying the criminal class as well as the police. Then, he extended his reach beyond, cupping the city at large in his cold calculations. There was nothing he could not do, nothing to stop him, so it had seemed.

The police did not admit it, but their lies were as bold on the page as Baum's own lies when he had call to use them. Luck, not the brilliance of the German Police, had been more at work in Dr. Mabuse's capture and subsequent internment. They supposed his mind had fractured into a scattering of neuroses. There, before Baum's careful eyes, was the real truth. Insanity was so very convenient. Besides, interned within a prison, wouldn't his almost unearthly intellect simply find more murderous souls to bend to his will?

No, the Asylum was much easier. There he could be observed and dissected until there was nothing left of the brilliant monster but more paperwork, more notes on a page. That is, if Professor Baum of the Berlin Psychiatric Institute could do to Dr. Mabuse what Dr. Mabuse had almost done with his plans to topple the German state, succeed.

* * * *

"Morning, Professor, " Nurse Harbou greeted him.

Baum nodded, still staring down at his documents. At the sound of her words, the print before him blurred into incomprehension. All that filled his mind at that moment was the image that had haunted him for days: the play of her elegant muscles as she walked away from him, down the shadowy corridors of the institute. The sharp, staccato sounds of her heels echoing with each step.

Finally after what felt like an eternity, he managed to stammer, "Good morning, Harbou."

"Did you have a pleasant evening?" she asked, standing by the corner of his desk as she delivered a new batch of documents. Absently, he noticed Mabuse's name on the top letter.

He had spent it in his empty house by the zoological gardens, immersing himself with more and more details of Mabuse's life. As the immense clock in the hall had rung twelve, one, then two, then three, he began to feel as though the genius monster's life was more real than his own.

Mabuse had graduated with phenomenal ease from Heidelberg, as a mathematics prodigy, at age fifteen. There was a lot about the young man in the files from the University, and while all of it praised his brilliant mind, they also formed a dark sink: admiration, but also some fear.

"His intellect shines through a darkness no man should know," one professor had written of his times with the young savant. Another scrap of paper coolly noted the same professor had jumped into the Rhine and drowned.

"Well enough. So much work to do. Kept me up most of the night."

"Would you like some coffee, sir?" she asked, turning to look back over her shoulder. Her lips were plush, a satin upholstery. Her eyes were shocking green, like priceless jade. Her skin was milk, still without a ripple or wrinkle.

"Yes, please," was all Baum could stammer.

He didn't want it. Not at all. Coffee gave him embarrassing diarrhea. But he wanted Nurse Harbou to get him something, even if it was something he didn't want.

"Cream?" she asked him. "Or sugar, Professor?"

He paused. "No, the coffee would be just fine."

Her bemused smile cut through him and he knew he had made a mistake. As the door closed, he caught a few bars of her jarring laugh. Hate burned his cheeks, but even humiliation didn't dispel the glowing nymph smiling sweetly in his mind, offering herself to him, to his power and dignity.

Mabuse became Doctor Mabuse in Munich, two years later. Two years unaccounted for, through the papers indicated that the police were still inquisitive. During his time in Munich there were several savage student riots, some even claiming lives. Documents indicated that the factions had been traced to two diametrically opposed groups in the city. Mabuse had been a member of both. It was as if he were conducting his own experiments, using the students in the school as A or B, the results being blood on the ancient city's streets.

The names and dates faded again, becoming nothing but scratches on yellowed paper as an image came unsummoned to his mind. Harbou, standing in his sad little bedroom, smiling. He, taking her coat. She, handing it to him with a seductively fluid motion. He, pouring peppermint schnapps. She, her perfect lips savoring the clear fluid. He, kissing those lips. She, next to him, the heat of her body warming him, arousing him. The sight of her bare breasts. The sight of her firm posterior in a sheath of silken undergarments. The feathery triangle of blond hairs between her strong thighs.

Mabuse had vanished from Munich in 1922, leaving behind nothing but the innocent debris of an average life. There were rumors. Forgery, extortion, assassination, murder... only rumor, supposition. In some cases Baum had detected an intentional illogic to the police's findings and theories. After all, the documents seemed to say, wouldn't it be better to feign ignorance than admit the true scope of his crimes?

Baum closed the folder and put his head in his hands. He only looked up when Nurse Harbou brought him his unwanted coffee — hot, and much too bitter — to thank her.

✶ ✶ ✶ ✶

"Do you know where you are, Doctor?" Baum said.

The man in front of him made no motion that he understood, but Baum knew he did. He sensed it, somewhere down deep.

Mabuse was a man, a fact he understood, having seen him in his cell every day since his arrest. But having him there, in the same room with him, the fact seemed somehow important. He was not ten feet tall, with eyes like lanterns blazing cruel brilliance. His hands were not misshapen claws, like some crippled despot. His body was not crooked to match his mind, like some Victor Hugo monstrosity. His hair was white, retreating from a domed forehead. His nose was pronounced, but not an eagle's beak.

His eyes … trying to explain, to categorize Mabuse's eyes, he failed. They were blue, almost like burnished steel, but even though they were hard and impenetrable, they were also immaterial. Instead of cruelly reflecting all they saw, they rather appeared to be ghostly windows into his unfathomably complex soul.

Mabuse said nothing. He sat, and he looked at Baum.

At first Baum felt suspense, expecting words to come. But then they didn't, and the Doctor's stare seemed to stretch into coupled eternities. At the first sight of Mabuse's eyes, Baum had looked quickly away, his inner depths burned by the Doctor's perceptions. But as the silence stretched, time slowed, and Baum felt himself … whither. Yes, whither, fade, dissolve away, simply from being in his presence.

Still, Baum held on as long as he could. Who are you? He thought, staring at the Doctor's chest. It was easier to take, somehow, reminding him of the criminal genius's flesh and blood needs with the faint rising and falling of his ribcage. What made you? What shaped you? What brought you into being? What sharpened your mind into a cruel knife? What burned you free of humanity? What gave you your power?

Baum was reducing, distilling. The world faded away until he was alone. He was just Professor Baum: small, fleshy, frightened, the illusion of intellect, the ghost of passion, dead of life.

The guard had to knock three times, loudly, before Baum pulled himself up from where he'd melted away. The spell was broken. The terrible presence faded as the guard entered, took hold of Mabuse's thick canvas restraints, and pulled him out the door.

Reflexively, Baum looked up to catch sight of Mabuse — from the back seemingly just a man as the Doctor turned to look back at him with those indescribable eyes. Then, he did what he hadn't done for the whole hour he'd been with Baum in his office. Mabuse slowly, methodically, blinked.

* * * *

"Nothing, Professor?" Nurse Harbou posed the usual question.

Baum wanted her. He wanted her aroused and passionate. He wanted to tear the starchy uniform from her, to relish in her body being revealed. He wanted to see the firmness of her breasts, the tightness of her belly, the gentle slope of her back, the dark red of her nipples, the blond silk between her legs. He wanted to listen to her throaty cries of desire. He wanted to have her, no, he wanted to take her. Then, there, in the dusty corridor of the asylum, her own musky perfume mixing with the harsh lemon of the industrial cleansers.

"No," he said, turning to look at her, his voice surprisingly even toned. "No change. None whatsoever. He eats what we put in front of him. He closes his eyes, so we presume he sleeps. But he doesn't move."

Nurse Harbou looked at him, quiet for a moment, as if seeing Baum in a new way.

"What is he?"

Baum felt the coolness that had descended on his soul break away, cheap glass flying to bits under the hammer of his desire for her.

"H..He is a man. That is all he is, " he said, shaking his head, as if trying to chase away the embarrassing stammer.

For the first time, Harbou seemed to diminish as well. When she spoke, her words were tinged with the musical lilt of a child.

"Maybe he's the devil, Professor."

"No," Baum said, sharply.

The devil could not be understood, the devil wouldn't give up his secrets, the devil couldn't be deciphered. He had to be a man, had to be. Only Mabuse, the man, would be able to explain what created Mabuse, the genius, the monster.

"He's a man. A special man, a man able to do what no other man could have done. But he's as much made of flesh and blood as you or me."

Harbou breathed in slowly, the action sending a hot flush of desire through Baum.

"Thank you, Professor," she said.

Then, she smiled an innocent, yet still sultry, display of silken lips and perfect white teeth before turning and walking away.

Baum wanted to watch her, to be obvious about his desire. He wanted to watch her walk away, relishing in the action of legs, posterior, back and arms. He wanted to watch her as a jungle cat watches a gazelle. But he didn't, because to his shame he was Professor Baum, so the instant she started to walk away he turned back to the solid iron door, the narrow observation slot.

Doctor Mabuse wasn't standing, as he had for months, in the center of his cell. He wasn't frozen, eyes glaring outwards.

Afterwards, Baum would wonder where he'd gotten the pencil, but right then the question never entered his mind.

On the white walls of his asylum cell, Doctor Mabuse was writing.

* * * *

"I am Mabuse. I am Mabuse. I am Mabuse…" the rest of it was illegible, though sometimes a word, or a phrase would emerge from the tightly compacted handwriting to stab out at Baum.

But that was clear, like a key function in a complex formula: "I am Mabuse. I am Mabuse. I am Mabuse."

Some of it was written where Baum could see it through the narrow observation slot in the door. But when the doctor moved to where he wasn't easily visible, Baum would wait an hour, sometimes two, before summoning the guards to have the doctor, as cool and remote as always, led away to a wait in Baum's office.

Then, Baum would enter and, under the harsh gaze of the single high bulb, he would read. Words would come and go, fading into the dense handwriting, surfacing in Baum's mind like the fin of some great shark in the normally placid waters of his mind. Like a dream suddenly remembered hours after waking, a meaning would surge into his consciousness.

But through it all, the one echoing sound, ringing through his mind was the constant: "I am Mabuse."

Had it been days?

Immersed in the words, Baum had neglected his empty house, his empty room, for a cot in his office. As seemingly inexhaustible as Mabuse himself, he spent every waking moment watching, trying to see as each loop and swirl was placed on the white stone walls, trying to pull meaning out of what Mabuse was writing. Hour after hour, he seemed to get closer and closer — or, as he sometimes thought as he paused to rub his eyes or drink some water — Mabuse was coming closer to him.

* * * *

"Professor?" Nurse Harbou said, standing next to him.

The asylum was quiet, the other inmates deep in their nightmares, dark night surrounding the world. Through the narrow slot in the thick iron door in front of Baum, Mabuse was meticulously scrawling out a new line to his opus. Ever since Mabuse had been brought back to his cell and locked in, he had seemed to be more driven to relay his words to the whitepainted walls.

Without pause for grammar, words flowed from his pencil. Some more than others.

"I am Mabuse."

"Yes, Nurse Harbou?" Professor Baum said, standing in front of the door, never taking his eyes off Mabuse and his words.

A new word seemed to leap out at him from the stream of code and rebus. The need to know tugged at Baum, hard — and then his key was in the lock and the door was opening.

"What are you doing, Professor?" the nurse said in alarm.

Baum turned quickly towards her.

"He's showing us, Nurse Harbou. He's showing us what's inside of himself, how he sees the world. No fear, no weakness — nothing but blinking perception. The world, his world, is crystal clear and certain. There's nothing that isn't possible — and no reason to ever hesitate."

Nurse Harbou's lips were soft, silken, strong against his own. She tried to pull away with a shocked word on her lips, but Baum was too fast, too strong. He took hold of her solid shoulders and pulled her back, forcing his lips again onto hers. Her hands, staccato, beat his chest but he knew — without hesitation, without doubt — that her body was responding, her protests were shallow, meaningless.

His tongue fought with her own, a humid wrestling in the hothouse of her mouth, a fight among the firmness of her perfect teeth, the softness of her cheek. He felt his body respond like it had never before — no torpid, guilt blushing erection, but rather a cool strength that reached down from his penetrating mind down to his manly physiology, creating for himself a determined, conquering arousal.

One hand on one side, the other on the matching, he gripped the front of her uniform, fingers brushing the buttons.

"Please..." she said, a softvoiced plea that might have been heard, once, as a bid for escape, but Baum knew it without hesitation to be a true plea for consummation.

The fabric vanished under his strength, buttons careening off the walls, to reveal a simple camisole of white satin. The reality of it, the undergarments of a woman, not a childish fantasy, amused him, and he laughed. The skirt was next, for he wanted to savor her pathetic arousal at humiliation. The fabric fell away, stitches popping quickly and neat, revealing a woman's panties. Again he smiled at the stains, the way they hung loose around her firm thighs, the way her pubic hairs pushed out at the thin material, and the growing spot of wetness.

Between thumb and forefinger, through the pitstained commonalty of her thin camisole, he pinched her nipple — hard. Her scream, shrill in the tiny room, echoed around them both, and a part of him enjoyed the complex harmonics and the way the sound seemed to sonically define the room.

She bent, hissing at the pain from his hand squeezing her nipple, arms flapping, as if the agony could be chased away like a threatening bee.

While he would have enjoyed simply seeing how much pressure she could take, there were other more interesting diversions that he suddenly felt the need to explore. The camisole had to go, and so it did. With a smooth economy of movement, he yanked the straps from her shoulders, and as she struggled clumsily to free herself of it, it slithered down into a small heap around her feet. Her breasts were aesthetically pleasing, plump and full, tipped with fat rings of areolae the color of rich flan. Her nipples were hard and obvious, pointing firmly toward the source of her arousal.

This time his hand dropped, finding the damp material of her panties. Cupping firmly upward, he pushed his thumb insistently ahead until it smoothly parted her lips, where he found her bead, the hot source of her passion.

He pushed, hard, upwards, and she moaned, deep and long, a thundering cry of outrage mixed with a hungry demand for more. Still solid and immovable, he pushed upwards again, this time carefully pinching one of her fat, wet, slippery lips. She bent, as if the strength had completely left her legs, until her head and her frantically panting mouth was against his chest. Carefully, skillfully — for hesitation and doubt were gone from his mind — he moved his hand so that two fingers were now ringing the tight muscles at the entrance to her vagina. Circling, teasing, causing her body to try and swallow the pseudocock of his hand, he felt her humid breath on his chest, the weight of her body trying to push itself down into his fingers. When he finally decided that it was sufficient, he thrust upwards, once, twice, three times until her moans became a deepbellied scream of release.

The orgasm electrified her muscles. She locked her hands around his wrist as she half insisted he stay in, and half demanded he pulled out. Her teeth bit down on his shirt, catching a few of his chest hairs in a distant flash of unimportant pain. He waited for her to catch her breath, but not long. Hands on her shoulders, he pushed her down, hard, 'til she was kneeling on the cold stone floor.

Freeing his cock was easy. His hands worked simply, elegantly, without a wasted movement, until his member was exposed. Without a thought, her mouth was on him, taking him down her tight, hot throat. Her passion was like a freed beast, something kept too long on a leash and then released to run wild. Strange, deep sounds seeped out from her full mouth — sounds of deep, earthen pleasure.

He watched her. There was desire, yes. He felt his body react, felt his blood flood. His semen became ready to emerge, but there was more there — a kind of ecstasy at having this woman in his control. He didn't have her body, he didn't have her sex, he had her — in his hand, to do with as he pleased. It was something he'd never felt before, a sense of elegant, perfect power, an absolute knowledge that he was totally, absolutely in control.

As his distant orgasm filled her mouth with sticky whiteness, he knew what and he knew who he now was — for it was the only thing that made sense, the only thing that felt right. Professor Baum couldn't have felt this way, he simply didn't have the ability. Therefore, he couldn't be Professor Baum. No, he couldn't. He could no longer be.

Picking up the sobbing woman, he led her out of the door of his cell and leaned her, a limp rag, against the cold stone wall. Then, he went back to room five, to where he knew he now belonged, and closed the door behind him.

* * * *

Where Dr. Mabuse had gone, how he'd escaped, no one knew. None of the guards had reported the patient leaving. For assuredly, they would have sounded the alarm. When the police arrived, they were shown the locked cell of room five by the dumbfounded asylum staff.

With eyes the color of cold steel, and at the same time clear all the way to the flickering brilliance of his twisted, brilliant mind, the man who used to be Professor Baum looked out at them. Unable to explain what had occurred, and unwilling to admit that Doctor Mabuse was once again at loose in the world, they simply locked the door to the cell, leaving his replacement to his endless writing on the white stone walls.

"I am Doctor Mabuse."

THE WATERS OF BISCAYNE BAY

If this story had a soundtrack it would be cool jazz, something with low, thoughtful notes trickling from a piano, and a slow, soulful sax. If this story had a texture, it would be soft yet scratchy like a vintage wool dress that's been slept in night after night. But if this story had a smell it would be nothing sweet or romantic. No perfume, no incense — nothing like that. Dead fish and motor oil. The look and the smell: Biscayne Bay.

The place wasn't what I expected, but then all I had was an old postcard to go by, and that had been taken at night. In the foreground a sweep of tiny blue lights marked the shore, dully reflected in the dark water. Some red ones, some yellow ones, and a couple of other colors, tiny points festooning the masts and bows of fishing boats. Miami was everything else: big hotels, neon signs, palm trees, and the gray curves of under and overpasses. High in the sky, there was a bright silver moon.

The reality was harsh and smelly. Dark water shimmered in gasoline rainbows; the tiny flashes of beer cans just under the surface. Guy wires ringing like bells on aluminum masts, swells farting and belching between old fishing boats. Why anyone would bother making the place into a post card was beyond me, and why anyone would ever come there even farther beyond.

At least I had a reason beyond inexplicable tourism. She'd talked about the place several times; she was fascinated by it. Something to do with that card she'd found somewhere and the lyricism of the name, Biscayne Bay. I guess she read too much Hemmingway in high school. Gail had always wanted to go there.

It was hot in the sun, so I tore my eyes off the scenic landscape and got back into my rental. A lot of the cool air had faded since I'd pulled up and gotten out, so I started it up again, cranking the AC up to arctic.

"What you expected?" I said to the cardboard box sitting on the passenger seat.

What would she have said? On the way down I'd superimposed her on the college kid sitting next to me, changing a pimple factory wearing headphones and bobbing to scratchy rap into an old lover. Bringing her back, at least in my imagination, was easier than going it alone.

"Not exactly the place for a golden moment, eh?" she would have said, laughing, smiling.

"Not even a brass one," I though.

"That's my darling, always the cynic. Your glass isn't even half empty. Instead it's broken, sharp pieces scattered all over, just waiting for bare feet."

"It just doesn't seem like a place worth capturing. To be thrown away, yeah, but not captured, even on a postcard."

"Whimsy, my dear Mr. Russell, is sometimes its own reward."

I was crying. I couldn't tell you when the tears had started, but there they were. I wiped them off on the sleeve of my jacket, blinking Gail away.

"Let's get a drink," was the last thing I imagined her saying. "Melancholy tastes so much better chased by a good scotch."

* * * *

Gail wore clothes. Simple cotton dresses, mostly. I remember one, a favorite of mine: short sleeves, pattern like a Japanese print, tiny blue birds chasing each other diagonally across it. Some magic of cut and seam made it move in special, mysterious ways: the buttons down the front parting here (a tiny window on white cotton panty), there (the swell of a breast), and other places (the plush pillow of her belly, the flat hardness below her throat, the momentary view of strong thigh). Gail wore clothes because she was always, and forever, naked under them. You and me, we're common human beings. We start at our slacks and jeans, gabardine and nylon. We start at our clothing, more comfortable with than without. Gail wore clothes, but they were never part of her. She hung them, tight in some places, loose in others, over her plush little body. You knew, looking at her, that they might fall away in an instant, discarded for what they were: just threads and shame.

Once inside the door they came off, dropped anywhere convenient or slipped slowly off of her. She'd walk, bedroom to bathroom, bathroom to bedroom, or even out to the backyard, and her simple cotton panties would slip, sag, droop and then fall down to her calves, then her ankles. With a kick, they'd fly off or just tumble away. She'd walk around her tiny house, the one her mother had left her, heavy breasts swaying with every step and movement. Going for a record (in the 80's) or a CD (after that), a nipple would peek, and then poke out. Putting it on the stereo (any decade), the other would follow. Suddenly aware of the confinement, she'd snort, say something silly about "bobby-traps" or something, and flip the contraption off. Or, taking aim with her tongue stuck out in concentration, she'd shoot it at a distant doorknob like some kind of double D rubber band.

Gail was a broad: sassy, quick, mercurial, fluid in her interests, slippery to define. Other women didn't like her, and she didn't like them.

"If you're going to bust balls," she said once, "don't pretend you're going to kiss them first."

I met her at a party a friend of mine had thrown, a little theme thing wrapped around a late night showing of *The Maltese Falcon* (in the early 80's, no VCR). I came as Bogart (badly), she came as Mary Astor (wonderfully). I knew my lines and she knew hers, and while the rest sat around a tiny television, we sat on the back porch and played our roles. Well, not expertly: Spade and Miss O'Shaughnessy/Wonderly/LaBlanc never kissed. We did. For what seemed like hours.

We never moved in together. We never talked about 'us', but we both knew that this was something good, something rare, and something magical.

It was quick, her death: a shadow on an x-ray, four months in a hospital, a small service, and a cremation. Boundless life to a small cardboard box on my car seat — all in half a year.

She left her house to me. I didn't want to go in, to start to dislodge any of the chaos that she'd created. I avoided it for months, until I was staring my fear in the face. The next day I rented a small van, and started dealing with the stuff of her life. It was easier than I thought. The CDs were just plastic and paper. The clothes were just — yeah — threads and shame. Then, I found the envelope, the envelope with the postcard and the letter.

I'd heard her talk about it, the waters of Biscayne Bay, but I hadn't done anything about it.

"Put me there," the note had said.

That's all.

Just "put me there" and that cheap, tourist shot of that polluted body of water.

And that's just what I'd do, after a good stiff drink.

* * * *

Gail loved the water. Mercurial, fluid, slippery, it was definitely her element. One memory stands out, a precious recollection I frequently fall back into now more than ever. It was a hot, sticky afternoon, maybe late July or early August of last year. My own little house, as always, was an oven, so I walked over to hers since I knew that hers was cooler. I found the front door wide open, and the house empty. In her tiny, carefully maintained backyard was one of those sprinklers that fanned water back and forth, back and forth. Lying on the close-cropped glass, naked but for a pair of cheap sunglasses, was Gail.

"I do declare, Sir, that this must absolutely be the hottest of days," she said, smiling, back of a hand to her forehead in a mocking swoon.

Gail wore clothes, but when she was free of them she was more alive than anyone I'd ever known. It was too hot for anything: eating, sleeping, walking, working — anything. Everything was slick with sweat. Even things that didn't sweat had a salty patina of sympathy.

Gail shone. Her wet body reflected the high sun, tiny reflections of it danced all over her. She was a voluptuous girl, with strong thighs, big breasts, a gentle belly, an ass like a pair of velvet pillows, and all of her glimmered with water from the sprinkler, glowed with sweat.

Watching me watch her, she smiled — making her dimples dance, her cheeks blush — and patted the grass next to her.

It was too hot to do anything, but I still took my clothes off and lay down next to her. It was even too hot to talk, each breath burning our throats, so we didn't. I just looked at her, and she looked at me, taking the sunglasses off and flipping them up onto the back porch. It was like I'd never really seen her before. The gentle rise of her belly, the way her breasts moved as she breathed, the color and texture of her nipples, the tangle of brown hair between her thighs, the way she pursed her mouth as she licked her lips, the feathers of her eyebrows, the perfect peach of her ass. I was excited, but it was too hot to get hard. We hovered there, lifted up by the so-hot air, suspended above arousal.

Even though my body couldn't respond, my mind did. My eyes touched her, relishing in her details, and the complete work of her they formed. We couldn't touch, couldn't talk, but we still made love. In the scalding gap between the sprinkler's warm rainfall, I watched her sweat mirror the sun. Sparkles played along the side of her plump breasts, gleaming on her strong thighs, shining on the curve of her neck. Then, when the water splattered down on us, I was hypnotized by the way the drops outlined her form, the way they raced down her breasts to hang under them, until they were too heavy and dropped to the green of the lawn. Watery jewels winked in her cunt's curly patch, forming a pool below, until there was too much and it trickled away.

We watched each other for hours, until the angry sun finally dropped below the peak of her roof. It never got cold, but it did cool enough for movement. My hand on her so-hot thigh, the water of the sprinkler, the water of her sweat making her almost frictionless, and her hand to my face. Her fingers were so hot I expected them to burn, but they didn't.

Slowly, as the air cooled, we moved more. She rolled onto her back, spreading her legs, and I lay my hand on that curl of wet hairs. Carefully, as if it was our first time, I explored. Our sweat never evaporated, and the sprinkler doused us, a fluid metronome. So it was a fluid evening time, a slippery dream night. She was wetter than I'd ever felt her, slick and hot beneath her tangle of brown hairs. Her clit was hard, a bead easy to find even in the falling night.

We stayed like that, the moisture of the sprinkler, the slickness of our sweat, the wetness of her cunt, enrapturing, hypnotizing me. I never found out if she came or not — the day was too hot for that — but I don't think it mattered to either of us. It was something other than just sex, it was something precious and sincere. A memory that to me, especially now, means Gail the way she was, the feeling of her soul, her spirit, primal, fluid, hot, and pure.

Thinking of her, thinking of that time, it was easy to summon her up again and imagine her sitting next to me as I drove away from the waters of the Bay, looking for a place to get a drink.

"If that doesn't scream then I must be deaf," I heard her say, nodding towards the first neon-lit place I saw: The Watering Hole.

I laughed, and pulled in between two sickly palm trees. It was her kind of place, comforting in its ordinariness, a place where they might not know your name but would still treat you like a friend in need of a drink. The cinderblock walls were built without even a concession to windows. The heavy swinging doors were reinforced with battered steel. A bright neon Bud sign buzzed angrily in a dirty Plexiglas box. The inside formed itself out of inviting dank as I blinked away the daylight: long bar, smoked mirrors, turgid fans, a jukebox that was gleaming and sparkling like some treasure from the cave of Ali Baba, and a chaotic solar system of tiny round tables with battered chairs for moons.

The bartender was a big redhead with a ready smile. He flashed it at me as I sat on a stool.

"Whatcha have?" he said as he absently wiped at the bar top.

Gail had joined me, making a comedic hop up onto her own rickety stool and turning 'vamp' up to full.

"Whatever you got, big boy," she would have said, a Mae West rumble to her already throaty purr. Would have … if she weren't in a box in my car.

"JB and coke," I said, smiling weakly at him.

"You got it. Gold and brown coming right up."

I could tell he wanted to talk, wanted to play the role of the bartender, but I didn't want to tell my story. It was too big, too raw to bring out — at least there. Instead I kept it locked up in my throat, somewhere close and personal, between a sob and a scream.

Instead of looking at him, I became fascinated with the bar's pattern of dark, dark wood. He got the picture, because a glass of ice and booze slid calmly into my view, no questions asked, no conversation started.

Sipping, I glanced up. I made her appear again, dressed in that special, simple cotton dress. She toasted me, winking, and the ache reached up and squeezed my heart. Pushing aside tears with the back of my hand, I looked up at the cash register. I breathed in slowly and deeply, trying to become fascinated by anything except for my memories and the big hole in me she'd left behind. Business cards and matchbooks, souvenirs from travelers and regulars, a "You don't have to be crazy to work here but it helps" sign yellowing and curled with age, a smattering of Polaroids: Red with someone who could be Jack Nicholson, Red with someone might be Mickey Rourke, Red standing next to a woman in a simple blue cotton dress, her smile bright in the gloom of the bar, someone I recognized immediately: Gail.

A picture of Gail and Red, smiling, standing together, taken right here, in a bar near the waters of Biscayne Bay.

✳ ✳ ✳ ✳

Sitting in the dark gloom of the bar, shook with pain and fury, my imagination surged against my will, filling me with images: Red kissing her, his thin lips matching her lush full ones. His hands dropped from her strong shoulders, down her arms, then to the small of her back. As the kiss intensified, as she moaned into his pressing mouth, he reached down and took hold of her ass and pulled her closer, tighter. She responded by grinding herself against him, trying to reach his cock through their clothing.

Then, their clothing was gone and she was taking him into her mouth, swallowing him deeper and deeper with energetic thrusts she slamming back into him as he thrust into her, both of them spitting and hissing encouragements.

The bar was stifling, hot. I was baking, burning inside. All I could do was sit and stare at him, at the picture, and, in my mind, at the two of them on that too-hot day, that special day. I could see them, clear in my mind, as they lay together on the grass, the beads of sweat and water from the sprinkler trickling down their sides. I watched as the water painted them with reflections, flowed down their sides, pooled in their navels, splashed over their faces, washing everything away.

We never talked about it, not really, but … I thought we understood that what Gail and I had was special, magical, precious, not something common, something not easily given away. More than sex, even more than languid summer afternoons full of sweat and water.

Anger battled with grief. My drink was long gone, just a thin mixture of water, syrup, and booze remained in the bottom of the glass. I couldn't bring myself to ask him to get me another. So I just held it, willing it to shatter in my tight grip, send glass flying everywhere, and into my hand. Maybe the pain would bring me out of it, blast the pain in my mind away with sliced skin and spilled blood.

But it held, and I held it. White knuckles and thick glass. I imagined her, sitting on a bar stool, holding his hand and laughing, sharing something much more intimate than anything we'd ever done. Biscayne Bay. I'd traveled hundreds of miles, spent so much time, just to find out that I'd never known her at all. The sex wasn't all of it — or most of it — hundreds of miles and days just to find out I wasn't worth telling the truth to. She'd been here before, been here before and been with him.

I finished the sickening remains of my drink and got up to go. As I walked, unsteady with booze and rage, I hoped he'd say something, anything, just to give me an excuse. To do what, I didn't know. Maybe punch him, smash the place up, cry or scream. But nothing happened. He didn't say a word. Silence followed me towards the door.

I'd go out, drive to the Bay, dump her ashes in, and leave, hopefully putting her somewhere where she couldn't haunt me again.

Then, she did. I turned, my hand on the cool metal door, and looked back. Red was doing something behind the bar, something involving the sharp clicks of half-empty bottles.

It wasn't right. I didn't know how, but it didn't feel right. There was something else, something hidden here, something about Gail, about Red, about the Bay.

I couldn't just bury her. Gail was worth too much to just throw her into that dark Miami water. I couldn't just get on the plane tomorrow and leave a Gail-shaped hole in me.

So I went back to the bar, ordered another drink, and then pointed to
the photo above the cash register.

"Tell me about her," I said.

* * * *

Deep night. Reality mirroring postcard. The distant chimes of guy lines
and aluminum masts, constellations of warning lights, bubbling tides
trapped by breakwaters, waves slapping against boat hulls. Gail was a water
woman and it was simply appropriate that she be returned there. Ashes to
washes, water to water.

The sea was dark and frightening. Looking more like oil than water,
each surge made it seem deeper, heavier. I parked next to a slipway, the
traction groves in the cement making it look like a deck of cards slid into
a pool of crude. I left my shoes and socks in the car, rolling my pant's legs
up to my thighs. Walking down, chips of concrete became tiny flashes of
pain underfoot. I was grateful when I got low enough for the sea to wash
over them.

The water was cold, surprising for Miami. A low shiver raced up my body
from my numb toes, feet, and legs, but I kept walking. Moving helped, and
my circulation vigorously pushed sluggish blood around, slowly warming
me. By the time the water was lapping at my stomach, I felt like I could have
left my clothes on the shore and swam out to one of the distant, sleeping
sailboats.

The sea reminded me so much of her. Even cold, I could see her on
that hot day, gleaming with perspiration and sparkling drops from the
sprinkler: a slick naiad, a sprite of fountains, waterfalls, and spring rain.
Yes: Mercurial, fluid in her interests, slippery to define. How could I ever
have thought I'd done it? I thought I knew her, thought I knew where she'd
flowed, what lives she'd splashed against.

Biscayne Bay. I'd asked Red to join me, to help me mix her with the sea.
He'd just shaken his head, slowly.

"You do it. She was a dream. I'd rather not wake up yet."

Poetic for a man who poured booze for a living, no wonder she'd talked
to him, listened to him, held his hand, touched him, made love to him.

We'd been special, Gail and I. They'd been special, Gail and Red. She'd
been in town one day. She met Red, a lonely, sad man who'd just lost his
wife in a boating accident. They talked; they spent a night of reassurance,
love, and hope together.

I'm glad she'd asked me with that postcard, that little note, to come here, to the Bay, trying to explain what had happened between her and Red, hoping I'd understand.

The bay lapped at me, surges from some distant ship leaving the harbor. The cold sea started to sneak my heat away, mix me with its dark water. I thought about saying something. In the end all I did was open the box and slowly spill Gail's ashes into the water of Biscayne Bay. Gone, but never, ever forgotten, by me, and by Red, and somehow that was more than all right.

WATERCOLORS

The Gold Man — what was what Javier, the doorman called him. Never to his face, of course. Never. Ever to the red cheeks, the firm stance, the precisely measured pace — to all that, and the yellow glimmers of his rings, the watch, the heavy belt-buckle, the thin chain around his heavy neck, it was always, perpetually: "Yes, Mr. Rootile," "Certainly Mr. Rootile," "Assuredly, Mr. Rootile," "This minute, Mr. Rootile," as the gentleman left or entered the green glass lobby of the Fernando Arms.

Hugo, the chauffeur, would echo this, in content if not in precise tones. His own bass Haitian sounding like an impending downpour as he sharply nodded to whatever Mr. Rootile said.

Though away from the cool confines of the Rolls Royce, away from the meticulous routine of the heavy Mr. Rootile, Hugo referred to him in the domain of his own private mind as Mr. Fog, a surprisingly literate reference to Verne's clockwise character.

To Mrs. Rootile he was 'husband' or, sometimes, even 'Dearest Randall'... though even the familiarity with his surname didn't give her any more comfort than anyone else who happened to orbit the man.

The staff of the Beresford Trading Company, to whom Mr. Rootile was the Chairman and President, he was one of two things: "Sir" to those having been employed for less than twenty years, and "Chairman" for the few who'd been there longer. Within the fields of his mind — where we will visit momentarily — Rootile considered it a testament to his love of humanity, his deep warmth for this earthly condition, that he allowed his staff the goal of "Chairman," and not hold them to the impersonal "Sir" for their entire tenure in his service.

The boys didn't have the benefit of knowing the man in the Rolls Royce in any other context save for his slow, idling rolling presence. Always in the early evenings, always coming from the far side of the wharves, down where the shadows cast by the Great Harbor Bridge made the cool nights by the piers actually cold. The large man in the fancy car was just a texture of their lives. To them, he was Mr. Money, a glittering patron of their charms, their beauty, their talents ....

To call them boys would be wrong, for that implies an innocence these young bantam roosters had long ago either sold or had stolen from them. 'Men' is also more inaccurate than truth — for they all had a well-maintained youth about them so, at first, it was easy to think them well under their linear or mental ages.

For them, the big man in the Rolls was a benefactor. For him, they hunted the used clothing stores for just the right pair of tight jeans, the only-slightly stained silk shirt. For him they practiced, trying to develop the right way to stand, the perfect smile, the most alluring twist of the eyebrows. Mr. Money didn't have a lot of it, by no means was he the most generous of patrons, but he was regular, reliable … and that was something precious in their often tenuous lives.

For the man in the Rolls, the man who fit "Mr. Money," "Mr. Fog," "Sir," "Chairman," or "Husband," the world was ordered and fit, because he made it so. For Mr. Rootile everything beyond his sight, his extensive reach, was chaos, a wildly spinning, out of control cosmos. He'd seen first hand what could happen if one allowed that turmoil to infect his life. On his mantle in his large apartments were two portraits on minuscule islands of dust so important they were to the order of his life that Mrs. Rootile never dared move them. Their austere faces staring out at him every morning — the slit eyes of Uncle Golta and the drawn face of Aunt Felice — reminded him of the pain that an unchecked and unordered world could bring, and the two small coffins behind them never let him forget the precious things an unchecked would could take.

Edwardo and Peppin had been more than nephews. They had been brilliance in an otherwise cloudy and tumultuous youth. Rootile hung onto his memories of their times together: swimming in the cold Turbach river, wandering into the dark woods, fumbling with their young bodies, first kisses, first feels, innocent questions answered with giddy enthusiasm with white knuckled determination. The flood that had claimed them — the sudden wall of water that had destroyed their school — had seemed so capricious, petty. As Rootile grew, he saw its thunderous potential anywhere, around every corner and in every unplanned event.

So he surrounded himself with order, a regimen of habits and expectations and so the waters stayed away. Though sometimes, if there was traffic, or something unanticipated knocked on the solid walls of his ordered fortress, he could hear the bubbling chaos of another flood looming.

* * * *

Not almost, not approximately, but exactly at seven every Monday, Wednesday, and Friday, Javier would see Mr. Rootile exit the gilded cage of the Fernando Arms elevator and make his way across the marble lobby. As he approached the heavy glass doors, Javier would open them, this would tell Hugo to mimic the same with the passenger door of the Rolls.

Monday, Wednesday, and Friday … pleasures of the body, Mr. Rootile felt and understood, were part of the human condition. But as with everything in his world, Rootile maintained a precise architecture with his bodily passions. Demonda, Mrs. Rootile, had a firmness and suppleness, curves that excited Rootile. Her performance in the bedroom was exquisite, perfectly matching his desires as he had planned and executed their courtship and marriage. Looking at her, even after ten years of domesticity, still filled his large form with steely passion. In their bedroom, he felt an exaltation that reached beyond his earthly form.

But each thing its place, and Mr. Rootile had other passions. On the drive over the Great Harbor Bridge, an action timed nearly to the minute, the touch always came to him. The city stretched out before him like a painting.

And, thus, thinking of paintings, he viewed the streets under the great span, and the young men who walked its hard gray streets as watercolors — Demonda was part of his life, permanent and fixed, so thus oils. The young men, though — they were watercolors, loose and temporary.

That day was no exception. Again the thought of art and paintings, which Mr. Rootile fell into with the regular comfort of his regular life. Again the descent down to the cool streets under the great bridge, and — again — the slow procession down those same avenues as Mr. Rootile made his selection for that afternoon dalliance.

The birds were on parade that day. As the day had been unusually warm, flesh tones were the theme. All along the street they stood or brazenly beckoned to the creeping Rolls. Viewed from the cool interior, warmed steadily by Mr. Rootile eager passion, their faces were like brilliant hothouse blooms: violet shading around their large, expressive eyes, bright reds glimmering from their pursed lips, exquisite rouge around their perfect cheekbones. Their clothing, too, was tropical rainbow plumage: scarves, wildly colored coats, pants so pale or tight as to appear nearly invisible, every possible hue of silken blouses and shirt.

Some, perhaps more brazen or simply more hungry, openly displayed their God-given charms, flashing pale globes of cheek or revealing impressive erections behind hands opened with a quick conjurer's gesture.

Then one of them, just one, caught Mr. Rootile feverish gaze.

Many reasons could have been behind Rootile's singling out of that one lad. He was striking for his simplicity. Where others were a riot of shade and hue, he was pedestrian in just denim pants, plain white shirt, dark sunglasses and heavy leather jacket. There was something else, a qualifier that Rootile couldn't articulate: innocence? subtlety? sensitivity? The words for what this lad conjured within him didn't exist in his vocabulary, but the feelings, yes, the feelings were present, powerful, and … hard.

A light tap signaled Hugo to stop. The instant the window descended, the birds flocked around the beautiful car kissing and making crude, vulgar and very direct propositions.

Against the immaculate colors of the British car, their tones turned shockingly cheap and Mr. Rootile's passion ebbed farther, faster than usual. What had been brilliance was altered to cheap and tawdry. Boas were bare of feathers, scarves were frayed and stained, blouses were absent of buttons and faded from too rough treatment. Their hunger, their cold determination, too, seemed harsh and angry as if instead of, as they proposition, sucking Mr. Rootile, they would have preferred to consume him utterly, leaving nothing behind of value.

Perhaps because of this that one lad, the simple one, stood out more. Unlike his gaudy, tawdry kin who swamped the car, he pulled back, leaning nervously against the rough, industrial walls. Something in his carriage, an arrogance tempted with a vulnerability, made Rootile want him all the more.

With a gesture honed from practice, Rootile made sweeping gestures, studiously avoiding eye contact with the other young men. Trained, they stepped aside with only a few scattered mumbles and feminine complaints. Pointing authoritatively — as only "Sir" and "Chairman" could — Rootile singled the lad out, then crooked that same finger in summons.

The young man hesitated, seemingly to wonder if it was, indeed, him that Rootile was gesturing to.

The other boys laughed at this, their sharp gaiety ringing down the street.

Slowly, the young man approached the fancy car.

Rootile opened a door, saying, "Get in."

Again — hesitation. A particularly loud boy, a flaming peacock of a young man, took the cautious lad by the shoulders and, laughing, pushed him into the cool interior of the Rolls.

Struck by this cruelty, Rootile caught the young man as he stumbled in and helped him to sit on the expensive leather next to him. With the shutting of the door, Hugo, his chauffeur, engaged the engine and drove away.

* * * *

"Don't be nervous," Rootile said, the ripples of anxiety that flowed through his passenger bringing out a tenderness that rarely surfaced.

The young man smiled, but it was still touched by a slight rigor of fear.

Rootile reached out a great tanned hand, shining with gold rings, placed it fatherly on his shoulders.

"You know what is expected of you?"

Again, a quick nod.

"Your performance will determine the size of your gratuity."

He looked away, coughed from a tickle of nervousness into a pale hand.

"If you understand the arrangement then we should begin."

Again, a ritual honed with endless, repetitive, practice, Rootile reached down and with a few tugs of his expensive leather belt, his Seville-Row suit pants, his immaculately precise fly, exposed himself.

His manhood, perhaps from the thrill of the new lad, perhaps from some quality unknown even to the meticulous and orchestrated Rootile, was full and engorged, a pale crimson member, uncircumcised so as to appear a thick-bodied candle, sans wick. Veins stood out along its length, thick cords of warm blood making Rootile's excitement even more obvious.

The lad looked even more nervous, even more scared.

Words came out of Rootile's mouth, a stream that — thinking back on that late afternoon in the Rolls — he would never be certain of their origin. Maybe words should have said on those warm summer nights on the riverbank with Edwardo and Peppin or maybe just words that the small child within the great, golden, Rootile had wished were spoken to him. Whatever the origin, the deep source, the fact remains that the older Rootile did speak to them, that afternoon in the great car.

"Do not fear me. There is nothing here that will hurt you. You are safe. If you wish, I shall ask my driver to turn about and return you. If you wish to be taken somewhere else, within reason, I shall even do so. What I ask is something that I would have of your own free will and no other way."

108

Reaching into his suit pocket, Rootile extracted a roll of bills.

"You interest me. There is something about you that excites me as few of the others have done. If you please me, I shall give you this. The choice is yours."

The young man looked at Rootile's firm, brown eyes and then at the thick roll of bills, then at the erection, still strong and proud springing up from Rootile's fine trousers.

Then, quickly, the lad nodded.

Still, there was hesitancy about the young man's attitude. He had agreed, that was certain, but — still — enthusiasm didn't light his eyes. Rootile grew concerned, not seeing the usual hunger that lit up the other men's eyes at the sight of his member and the money.

But then the young man scooted along the fine leather seat and, still tentatively, he gripped Rootile's cock with one slender hand.

The touch, to the Golden Man, was electric. There was something about this lad, something beyond his watercolor Monday, Wednesday, Fridays, something special. That specialness seemed to radiate between the two of them and, even though the lad's anxiety was obviously still present, it also seemed to reach out and touch him as well. His hand was firm and strong, not with the usual "performance" that Rootile found in too many of the lads. There seemed to be a real fire about the young man as well as that touch of fear.

Then, just as Rootile was beginning to have his own fear (that the young man was never going to use his lips), the fellow did exactly that. With a sensual shock of wet silkiness, he dropped his mouth down and, though still with a shy hesitancy, some refined enthusiasm. The swallowing was done expertly, a steaming embrace wrapped with lips, tongue, and throat about his throbbing cock. The contact was more than electric, more than just a physical meeting of mouth to member. There was something pure and special about the meeting, one that sent almost-violent tremors of pleasure through Rootile's grand body.

As the young man worked at him, their mutual soft, low moans mixing into a kind of two-pant deep harmony, an image danced up from within Rootile's then-busy mind: the image of the youngster's body, naked, shining with a gleam of sweat, his own member large and firm in Rootile's dark hand. The image grew more and more firm, real, desired with the pulsing lips on his cock until Rootile thought he would burst or seize with frustration.

So enraptured was he with the image, that he placed a hand on the lad's head and gently disengaged him from his throbbing cock. Then, despite the feeble frustrations of the young man, Rootile started to undress him.

Strangely, two forces seemed at work within his paid companion, one was a brilliant fear that Rootile should touch him, and a desire, seemingly, that the patron do exactly that. While thin, delicate hands batted at Rootile's tanned ones, they did not beat anywhere near their obvious strength, ferocity.

Rootile was beyond reason. He had taken a brief trip beyond the walls of his rational castle. He had ventured far from its predictable gates and, instead, was where flood waters seemed to lap too close, too powerfully. This he knew. He was well aware, but his desire had taken control of him, seized him in a firm grip of feverish dream. The young man, his proud member tall and straight, golden skin, a passionate dew making his boyish body gleam … yes, his member –

The flood waters, threatening in the distance, became a mighty, heady roar as Rootile finally undid the young man's pants, finally lifted his white t-shirt.

No bronze chest with lovely seams defining strong pectorals, no youthful strength, no whip-cord muscles. Softness. Curves, no straight edges. It wasn't disappointment that stormed through Rootile as he uncovered the secret … it wasn't fear, and it wasn't anger, but, rather, stunned shock when Rootile realized that his boy, the young man that had been pleasuring him so perfectly, wasn't a boy at all.

Stunned, shocked that his ordered life wasn't so completely ordered after all.

* * * *

The ride back was done in heavy silence. Not the most talkative at the best of times, Rootile sat in the luxury of his back seat and allowed himself to be conveyed home.

After all, it was a Monday — and like every Monday, Wednesday or Friday Mr. Rootile would go to the bridge, would receive a service from one of his watercolor boys, and then would return. It was his ritual, his structure, his world.

Today … should have been no exception. The telephone in the back seat, normally would have been in Rootile's hand with orders streaming out of him and to his agents on the other side, orders delivered with crisp authority from a refreshed and satisfied man. It was, instead, ignored. Its soft purr continued as Hugo drove, its unexpected presence profoundly disturbing.

More breaks in the pattern… Rootile stared out the window, seemingly fascinated by the buildings blurring by. His eyes seemed larger to Javier, as if opened for the first time, either that or wide with fear. For Hugo, the chauffeur, it was hard to determine.

All the way across the bridge, all the way down the rich streets, all the way to the usual, the expected, the predictable, Hugo drove his master home.

∗ ∗ ∗ ∗

When he got there, even the stable castle of the Fernando Arms did little to soothe the turmoil within Mr. Rootile. Exiting the plush armor of the expensive car, accepting the punctual and precise movements of the dedicated Hugo, the Chairman's mind was not following its own familiar pathways, its own well-known corridors. No, he wasn't walking the lush carpeted hallway. Rootile wasn't strolling the familiarity of 21 to 22 to 23 to, finally, his own 24. He wasn't fishing in his well-sewn pockets for the well-recalled tune of his keys. No, he was still in the back seat of his plush English car, still expecting a penis and instead seeing femininity, wanting masculinity and discovering a young girl's genitals.

The world wasn't as he thought it to be. The reasons could have been many, varied (a prank, a sister being with her brother, a desperate woman … many, varied) but none of them came to Rootile's mind as he turned the key in his lock, pushed open his door. Instead, all Rootile thought, dwelled upon, was that his sphere, so complete and ordered, was now completely uncertain, chaotic. The waves of that impending flood had crashed upon his ramparts, and shown his castle walls of order to be figments of a very-insubstantial imagination.

Within, his wife — honed to ordered perfection — greeted him with a chaste kiss and a snifter of fine brandy. On the table in his study was a copy of the evening's paper, a sharpened pencil, and an apple on a fine china plate. What she did during this hour, the time it would take Rootile to read the news, mark anything of interest to the Beresford Trading Company, and have his slight snack, was a mystery to him.

At the door, he hesitated. Uncertainty gripped him. The world wasn't ordered. It was fragments and parts. It wasn't expected, wasn't known. What strange things could his wife be doing during the time it took him to leisurely read the *World Herald*?

Standing there, the ghostly expectation of a man's penis and the real sensation of small, budding breasts in his hands, Rootile was seized by a quick fear, a suspicion that the walls around him were not just insubstantial, his illusions designed to trick him, to deceive.

111

Turning, he gripped his wife's pale, slender shoulder and pulled her in front of him. Shocked by the break in the rituals of the house, Demonda gave a sharp sigh, a sound normally heard during their times in their great bed.

As was her own habit, Demonda wore a simple chiffon dress, a ghostly gown of soft silk.

Through it, distantly, Rootile was aware of her nipples hardening.

As it was soft material, it came away quickly, parting with only a few precise, yet fevered manipulations of Rootile's big hands. A bow there, a strap slipped over a slender shoulder. Inch by quick inch, it fell away. Images danced through Rootile's mind as he hurriedly undressed his wife, visuals of laughter at finding a young boy in her place, of finding not full breasts tipped by knotted nipples but rather a ribbed chest, not a downy pelt between her legs but rather a strong member to rival his own.

Bow, strap, naked she stood in the doorway. She seemed to glow, to pant with quick, shallow breaths. The unpredictable in the ordered Mr. Rootile exciting her beyond any forbidden fantasy, filthy sin.

Her excitement came to him in a barrage of senses. Her nipples stiffened more than their usual when aroused, the scent of her sex heavy in the stale air of the apartment, the way her legs bent just so as if preparing for a descent onto his still-obscured cock. Without his direct will, his hand dropped down her slight belly, tickled through the hairs on her mons, parted her wide lips and found a practical sea of moisture.

To this, Demonda sighed deep and long, a single musical note that Rootile had never heard before. One of her hands dropped to the front of his trousers and found as much a surprise to Rootile as to her, a ready and strong cock.

The orders, the structure was simple and pervasive. With the young men it was the mouth, the lips. They were his watercolors, his pleasure of that flesh. They were the world of pleasure. For Demonda, she was of her other lips, of the marriage bed and the transcendence of the self through intercourse.

For Rootile, the twain had never met, never crossed the line he had so vigorously drawn.

On one side the firmament of marriage, on the other, the watercolors of young men.

Demonda knelt, pulling down the zipper on her husband's fly as she descended. Her fall was slightly hesitant, as if she expected to be vigorously pulled upwards against the forbidden pleasure. Rootile's hands, instead, fell gently to her cool shoulders and eased her onto the red carpet.

Much churned through Rootile's mind: fear at the falling of his ramparts, the ticklish terror of the unknown; the expecting crashing of waves, the surging death of fast-racing waters; and the flaming hunger of his body, of the breaking of the chains that had held him trapped to intercourse with wife: lips on member only on Monday, Wednesday, Friday afternoons. The forces bashed against each other, fear and liberation, sorrow and hope.

Demonda's hands reached within and after a few deft manipulations, managed to extract his member. Once freed, she wasted no time, no hesitation, in wrapping her own silken lips around his burning-warm cock. The sounds that slipped beyond the flesh of her husband's penis within her hot mouth were ones that neither of them had heard before, a vocabulary unspoken in the ordered routines of their lives.

Back and forth, as rehearsed in too many dreams, her head and lips worked at him. Rootile, lost in the turmoil of his cracking world, felt the pleasure as a fluttering brilliance at the edge of his anxiety, his fear. Slowly, though, it pushed aside every other feeling within himself until it consumed him. The world, right then, was just his wife's hungry lips consuming his pulsing manhood.

The orgasm came. There was the physical, yes; the jet of salty thickness in his wife's mouth, the hungry swallow afterwards, the rushing pleasure through his body, the quaking of his legs, the shiver of delight; but there was also a brilliance, a shining light.

Somehow, details lost against most important events, they came to be as husband and wife in bed, Demona curled against his dark body, her tresses falling over his arm.

Sleep claimed her first, slipping her down into a rocking domain of fragmented dreams. Mr. Rootile, though, he laid awake as long as possible — holding back heavy sleep. There, in that time between his own dreams and hard reality, he listened very carefully: the creaking of the great building, the far off sounds of the nighttime city, the warble of a distant radio ... but no matter how hard he listened, he could not hear the waters, the heavy waves.

As dreams did come, he smiled at the fact that they might never arrive, after all.

AMAZON

It was the middle of the night, after Fala Lalafaluza's opening pink feathers act, but before Amazonia's whip-cracking to *These Boots Are Made for Walking*, and Valerie VaVoom closing bare bush special. They were all up there, the three headliners of the Black Cat Club and a few assorted girls digging for their own twenty-minute sets in the spotlight. The Parade is what they called it, and sometimes it was fun, seven or so girls bouncing their tits or swinging their asses, boas sweeping the stage in slow motion, glitter scratching underfoot, trying to work out some kind of chorus line to a current top ten tune.

It was halfway through the fifteen minute set, eight girls kicking up their legs, shaking their tits, when it happened.

"Sorry, shorty," Claire — Amazonia — said in a thunderous stage whisper after her muscular thigh smacked hard into Vivian's face, sending the dwarf tumbling to the stage.

Fala quickly bent down and helped Vivian back to her feet. This got Fala a smoldering look from Claire, who cracked her whip, sending the girls on either side of her skittering away.

When *Sugar, Sugar* finally ended, Vivian knelt down and retrieved her boa. From the opposite side, Fala watched her for a few seconds, until Claire, a scowl on her thin face, looped her whip around Fala's neck and violently pulled her towards the dressing rooms.

When the lights finally went down, the last person on the stage was little Vivian, until she stepped quickly off into the wings.

✷ ✷ ✷ ✷

"Fucking bitch," Claire said.

She was standing by the door, which was closed, whip still in her hands. The cheap leather creaked as she flexed it.

"She's disgusting. She's just here to laugh at, but they're laughing at us, too."

"Oh, yes, Claire … I know."

Fala was wearing only a silk dressing gown, and her full figure swayed beneath the thin fabric. She stood, leaning back against her backup table, with the same sensual grace she brought to the boards, the same almost-innocent poise she used when she took off her clothes to a hall full of heavy-breathing men.

In a hall of cheap feathers and glitter, Claire, though, was cheap leather, buckles, and fishnet. While the other girls stripped down or slipped on comfortable, sensible underwear as soon as their acts were over, Claire kept her leather, buckles and fishnet on until it was time to step out into the early morning — and then sometimes she'd simply throw a heavy raincoat on over it all and walk out, not changing 'til she got back to their apartment, if then.

Claire still had her whip, still stretched tight in her hands, but as she eyed Fala, the twisted leather sagged, just a bit.

"Yeah, Fal, you know."

The handle end dropped, then the thin end, until the whip was a sloppy coil on the floor.

"Tasty," Claire's voice was low and gruff as she reached out and slowly, carefully opened Fala's gown, revealing by fractions the swell of her breasts, the pushy swell of her belly, the few brown strokes of down between her legs, and then, as the silk slid over her shoulders and to the floor, the twin pink knots of her tightening nipples.

"Very tasty indeed." Claire said, gazing down at Fala's full, rich body. "Oh, yeah."

She reached down and pushed her fingers between Fala's thighs, until Fala took the hint and, with a sigh, walked her feet apart, opening herself.

"You understand, don't you, doll? She's a fucking joke, right? She's a freak, they laugh at her. So when we walk out there they laugh at me, too."

Claire's fingers pushed, hard, up and into her cunt.

Fala started with "Claire…" is a firm tone, but then didn't say the next word, or the next, instead substituting "Whatever you say, Claire."

Never taking her hand out, Claire slowly eased herself down into a squat in front of Fala's tangle of pubic hair.

"So sweet," she said, as if she were speaking to Fala's cunt and not the cunt's owner.

Her hand started to move, slowly at first but then faster and faster, until her clutch of fingers were blurring in and out of Fala's cunt.

As she fucked Fala, Claire mumbled: "Sweet fucking cupcake sweet fucking slit sweet fucking slut sweet cup sweet cake…"

It took a little clumsy effort, but eventually Claire got her own fingers into her own cunt, pushing her right index deep inside, thumb pressing and circling her own throbbing clit.

Above, staring out into space, Fala grunted. Each thumping out of her chest to Care's rough thrusts, hips moving back and forth in synch with the deep sound. She noticed a bit of feather on the top of her right breast and, without breaking the rhythm of her hip-sways, reached up and carefully plucked it off.

Below, lost in the actions of fingers in Fala's cunt, fingers in her own cunt, Claire reached boiling point. Her face and body was covered in a thin layer of salt and feverish excitement. Her eyes flickered from one tiny sexual detail to another: the way Fala's mons was thick and padded, the way her slit open/closed with each thrust of Claire's fingers, the gentle swell of her belly, the shadows of her big breasts cast by the overhead lights; until with a single, very hard press, she pushed herself up and over into a shuddering, gasping come.

Breathing quick and sharp, Claire lost her balance, tumbling away from Fala's cunt. With a less-than-dignified impact, Claire's ass hit the floor where she sat for a moment, then two moments, gasping in ragged breath.

"Cupcake," she finally managed to gasp, smiling deliriously starting up with wide eyes at Fala.

"Yes, Claire … cupcake," Fala said with a furtive smile.

Then, she closed her robe and extended a hand to help her lover to her feet.

* * * *

"–so the wife says, 'Honey, this one's eating my popcorn.'"

Their laughter was hard, deep, fast and true, and Fala felt a quick smile flicker across her lips even though she'd only heard the punch line and not the set-up.

As Fala pushed through the curtain, she saw one, two, three of the girls — Bunny, Doris and that skinny little girl who also worked the front cash register. They were all sprawled out, eyes sparkling, as little Vivian held court backstage, shoulders back, purple boa tossed over one shoulder, somehow stately in miniature garters, fishnet hose, black panties, black satin bra.

"Now go on, my pretties!" Vivian cackled with theatrical glee, "Go out into that dull, dull world and shine with your delightful brilliance. Go on, beat it ya bums!"

Laughing, the girls floated away, every one of them tossing a "good night, Vi," or a "sweet dreams, Vi," or even a "love ya, Vivian" as they walked past.

"What a great bunch o' gals," Vivian said, laughing lightly, one leg up on one of the crates, a miniature Blue Angel.

She adjusted her boa, stretching it out as if inspecting it for missing feathers.

"Something I can do you for?" she said, her eyes penetrating Fala.

"I just wanted to … Well, I'm sorry. For Claire. She can just be really … difficult sometimes."

She found it hard to look the dwarf in the eyes. Vivian laughed, quick and short, hopping off the box and strutting towards her.

"No big deal anyway, besides, for all that leather and shit I bet our Miss Amazonia is a really pussycat, right? Bet she even has some kinda silly pet name for you, right? Lemmie guess, something cute and frilly, right? Something like … Kitty? Princess? Sweetie? Cookie? Cupcake…"

Fala twitched, a blinked, took a short breath. The dwarf beamed. Vivian's face lit up as if caught in one of the spots.

"Knew it! Oh, man, that's rich. But, you know, that's also a little sad 'cause you're not sweet."

Vivian's eyes narrowed as she stepped even closer to the stripper.

"Nah, you're nasty, aren't you, girl?"

Vivian's hand, somehow, was on Fala's meaty hip. And, *somehow*, Fala didn't mind. Her face felt uncomfortably warm, like a bourbon blush on her cheeks, and she found her legs aching, just a bit, as if she had either run a mile, or was just getting to.

"Nah, you're not sweet. There's nothing innocent, nothing precious about you."

Conveniently close to Vivian was of the crates, and Vivian nimbly hopped up on it putting her face close to Fala's.

"No, Fala, I know what you really are. You radiate it. You reek of it. You're a slut."

Vivian was short, small, squashed down, maybe four feet high, and that was being generous. Her legs were stumpy, her feet like plump miniatures of real feet. Her arms were the same, bulbous in some places, like adult muscles on a child's frame. But Fala's nipples were aching, her lips were slightly parted and as if it were happening to someone else, she was aware of her cunt's steady pulse.

All kinds of words were trapped in Fala's throat. Too many of them, with diverse meanings, everything from "no!" to "more!" so her body was left to respond on its own. She nodded her head.

"I knew it. I knew it straight off. A true blue, all-the-way-to-the-core slut."

Her voice dropped down low, so Fala had to bend down slightly to hear each word:

"And there's nothing better than a slut."

The kiss was sudden, hard and good. One minute Fala was stretching her ears to make out each word and the next their lips were together.

Pain made Fala break the kiss, a sudden, sharp shock. Looking down, she saw that Vivian had deftly parted her robe and was expertly pinching her left nipple. It was right, perfect, not enough to make her pull away, but hard enough to bring tears to her eyes.

Fala felt her legs grow weak. She collapsed back against another of the crates. The word had shrunken down to her cunt, aching, and her nipple, aching, and Vivian's voice.

"You live for your cunt, don't you? You have nice eyes, Fala. Real nice tits, real good lips, a wonderful laugh, damned fine legs, but your cunt. Ah, you're cunt is a marvel, a treasure, a prize."

No hesitation but with also no hurry, slowly, savoring every inch, Fala swung her legs apart, exposing her downy hair, her plump, swollen lips.

"That's why you get out on that stage, to show that pretty, pretty cunt to the world. But showing it just ain't enough is it? No, because a real slut can't just show off her cunt."

With a quick hop, Vivian was back on the boards, standing between Fala's spread legs. Focusing from her pulsing lust, Fala saw the little woman staring at her with pure malicious intent. It was something she'd never seen before. Control, power, will, all packed in feathers and frills and no more than four feet tall.

Vivian's hands were small, but not child-like. Even though she couldn't exactly see what she was doing, Fala instantly became an admirer of her skill. It was as if a brilliant conductor was playing her cunt. Fingers tracing her slick, plump lips, dipped in just enough to break the seal and allow her hot juices to flow. A tap — then several taps — fell on Fala's heart-beating clit. Soon Fala was hissing. Then, she was moaning. Then, she was panting. Then she was doing all, together, at once, as Vivian spread Fala's moisture all over her cunt with deft touch.

"But you are a special slut, aren't you, Fala, because you don't want to just be filled, right?"

Vivian's words were growls, deep thunder, and Fala could do nothing but nod in response. Then, there was pain, a blinding burst of light behind her eyes.

Reflexively opening them, Fala glanced to see Vivian's hand on her left nipple, savagely twisting the sensitive brown tip.

"Say it, slut, be proud of what you are!"

From somewhere deep, Fala knew what she wanted, more than anything. Proudly, in a voice that shocked herself with its volume and determination.

"Yes! I'm a slut. Fuck me!"

"Anything you want, slut," Vivian said, her rough voice dripping with playful sarcasm.

Her hands were small, but they were absolutely, positively, perfect for fucking, which is what Vivian did to Fala. It was a hard driving fuck that thrilled Fala from her outer lips to the deep insides of her cunt. It was a fuck that made her ass scoot back and forth on the crate, made her nipples ache, a fuck that made her moan, sigh, pant, and all of that and much, much more.

Then, she came, with a crash and a cunt spasm that locked onto Vivian's hand like a handshake. Smiling broadly, Vivian remained between her legs, hand firmly up inside Fala till the bigger woman's contractions and moans boiled down and down and down to a blissed out smile on her sweat-shimmering face.

"T-thank you," Fala managed to say as she slipped down, collapsing into a pieta of frills and feathers.

Vivian walked around the crate and, bending down, kissed her, a sweet, innocent, rewarding meeting of lips on lips.

Then, in a simple, honest voice, she said, "Anytime, slut. Anytime at all."

* * * *

"Hey, Fal, get out here. They're closing up. Get your fat ass out here!" Claire said, standing at the top of the aisle, hand on the door to the lobby.

She was dressed to leave, heavy topcoat over her patent leather, whip coiled like a belt around her waist.

"She'll be right out," Vivian said, sprightly jumping down off the stage.

She also was dressed for the outside world: tight blue jeans, white t-shirt, leather vest, and biker boots.

Claire didn't respond with words, but her face tightened into a stone mask of displeasure. It was like she wanted to say something but couldn't.

Then Fala came out from the dressing rooms. She looked at Claire, a quick, glance, and then at Vivian, smiled and gently dropped her eyes.

"Hey, you coming or not?" Claire said, voice trying to be strong but instead coming out strident.

"No, bitch, she's not," Vivian said, her words thundering in the hall. Then, softer, to Fala: "Come along, slut."

Fala smiled, wide and true and took the tiny woman's arm. They pushed open the side door and stepped outside, Fala saying "Yes, Master" as the door swung shut behind them.

THE CURSE

Blood on the sheets.

When she awoke, blood on the sheets.

Not a lot, but enough. Even though she was alone, embarrassment warmed Ellie's cheeks as she stripped her bed and tucked them into the laundry hamper. At least they hadn't been new.

Alone?

Slowly, memories surfaced past the beginning of her daily routine. Showering, washing herself, she remembered other hands... there, there, and there.

The night before?

As crimson spiraled away at her feet, down the drain, it seemed to be replaced by a quick storm of recall: the thumpa, thumpa, thumpa of the band on a distant stage, the biting sting of clove cigarettes and ganja in the air, the distant frostbite of a very cold beer in her hand. It was the perfect place, a lovely excuse — women everywhere, dancing under a painfully blue sky and then under hard industrial lights. Pride Day — a time to step out, wear the colors, be free. A special women's space, on a special gay day. But...

Ellie had felt uncomfortable. For a while she'd watched, marching the route with the rest, becoming a part of the crowd. But then the isolation returned and she was just one among thousands. Just a face in that overwhelming crowd.

She recalled the depression, like a heavy blanket around her shoulders. So many women dancing around the outdoor stage, a parade of their own, all the pretty young girls moving with each other. Smiles, laughter. And all she'd wanted, desperately wanted, was someone to be with.

Company... Then someone had, someone had stepped in. A quick cascade, an explosion of fire-hued hair, huge dark eyes, lips that seemed to slyly smile from the poster of some silent-film queen, a lithe form, slender and graceful under the pulsing lights, the harsh street lamps, the tiny bulb of her car's feeble dome light, the harsh fluorescents of her lobby, the glow from her familiar lamps, then — lastly — the contours of her illuminated by the ember-red numbers of her night stand clock.

Twisting off the shower she stepped, wet and dripping into the bedroom, hoping for her, hoping to see her elegant eyes, brilliant lips, deep-throated laughter.

But only covers on the floor, only a bare mattress waiting for her.

Alone? Yes.

* * * *

She was almost late coming into work. Unheard of, though no one would have noticed. She'd stood and stared at the bare bed, looking for some kind of evidence, some kind of physicality to match her filling memory.

They'd stood on the balcony, looking at the stars and the brilliant lights of the city. A natural position, Ellie's hands on the cold metal of the balcony, the other woman's hands around her waist, her breath on the nape of her neck. A cascade, Ellie remembered, of goosebumps, but not from the cooling night.

Hard daylight. Blinking, wrapped in a towel, she stepped out, looking for footprints, hand prints. Moisture, a sparkling flicker of dew, anything to prove it had really happened.

They'd kissed. Yes, and she tasted her again in memory, the pressure of lips, the heat of her, the rhythm of their breathing. They'd come inside, kissed by the foot of the bed. The whisper of her black satin dress, the sudden too-tightness of Ellie's jeans. The surprising laughter when the kiss broke, when the high of their excitement crested. The way, then, the giggles had faded as she had put her hands on Ellie's face, traced the contours of her cheeks, her jaw, the way she'd tapped Ellie's nose, whispering "button" in a rich, throaty voice.

In the warming room, Ellie stood at the foot of the bed, turning so she was facing the way she remembered standing. Yes. Eyes brown with flickers of amber. Lips too full, too red, too silken to be anything but a fantasy running around in the real world. Lithe, boyish. She remembered how she liked to watch her move, liked to watch her walk barefoot across the apartment. Graceful, as if every muscle were elegantly conducted to some lovely score.

Her shoes?

Yes... She'd kicked them off, near the foot of the bed. Without really thinking of the woman walking the hard pavement on thin, bare feet, Ellie dropped down to look, hoping for the reality of a simple black pump. Nothing, of course. Memories, but nothing else.

A glance at the clock brought up more — her face, glowing as if from low embers, smiling up at her. There, in her eyes was the lust Ellie'd wanted, needed, but also something else, something finer, softer, kinder. There was something else there, in the dull red glow, something that had made Ellie's heart melt as fast as her body. Liquid — yes, molten...

A glance at the clock also brought a slap of reality. 8:05. Half an hour on the bridge, fifteen minutes from the garage to the office. She was going to be late.

Still, hurrying, there was no escaping the growing number of ghosts from the past, that expired night: brushing her hair brought up a voice, rich and rumbling, and the feel of strong fingers stroking the top of her head; doing her teeth was those same fingers brushing her lips, feeling them before another kiss...

Finally, she had to stop, had to put both hands on the edge of the sink and breathe deep. In and out. Strong, steady breaths. She was late, she needed to get dressed and get going. She had work to do, lots of work to do. If it had happened … if it had happened then it was nice, and that was all. It didn't change anything. If it hadn't, then the world was as it was.

Ellie, her little place, her little life, her job — the days falling down, one by one.

Tears, hot on her cheeks. How she wanted it to be real.

Eyes open, puffy and red. Her face in the mirror, looking broken and small.

But then she saw it, as real as a shoe, as foot and hand prints in night dew. Evidence, reality. Purple and harsh, sore, yes, but evidence none the less. A scarf would hide it, but not for now. Lateness, the bridge traffic, the walk from the garage, the firm, everything was gone from her mind. For now, as she stood in the window, the bruise on the slope of her neck was too priceless to hide, too real not to be stared at.

* * * *

The office normally seemed to exist out of time. One day there melded into the next and then the next, usually, as an endless caterpillar of files, meetings, filings, a slow dance of meaningless movements that seemed to have no function aside from filling days.

She'd smelled of lemons, strong and sharp. A bite to the nose, a sting as they'd kissed. Ellie was opening her first file of the day when the memory came, strong and fast. In an instant, she felt her body respond. Though shame bloomed on her face, she relished the new information, a few more details to the mystery.

She usually made small talk with the others, television of the night before, the day's headlines, something safe. But that day she walked through the office like a woman still asleep, lost in her vivid recall.

Lemons, she thought, accepting another load of papers, and hair... hair the color of rusted wire, a brilliant halo of light.

"Sure, no problem," she said to someone who stuck his head into her office, his face a mask of seriousness. She had no idea what she agreed to, her lips forming the dismissive words just to get him gone, to get him to leave them alone, just Ellie and her slowly dawning memories of the day before.

Jennifer, the little, bob-haired girl from Shipping, stopped by when the clock was inching towards five, wanting gossip, both to pick up as well as give.

"What did you do after the parade, hum?" she said, implying, suggesting, mocking because she suspected the answer was nothing.

Ellie wanted her gone as well. How do you put the bite of lemons, hair the color of a sunset, into dyke drama? Even bringing the woman up with Jennifer would be a kind of sacrilege, a Polaroid of Jesus on the cross.

Instead, she smiled her best fake smile and said, "Not much."

The night didn't share anything else. The bed was just a bed, still no shoes shoved under, still no palm-prints on the railing. Only the mark on her neck, the fading reddish bruise, was all that remained, and even that seemed to be healing, fading into just plain skin.

∗ ∗ ∗ ∗

Her voice. The sound of it, the ringing timbre of her speaking, washed over Ellie as she opened the Peterson file. So strong, so realized in her ears, Ellie had to close her eyes to focus on its clarity. A lilting voice, full of honey and wine, with a touch of somewhere South, but not corn-pone. More white-painted mansions and the kindness of strangers.

"You from around here?" Ellie had said, regretting the stupidity of the line the instant the words had stumbled out of her mouth.

"Sometimes..." she'd answered, conjuring bayou and Savannah, with a brilliant smile. "Want to dance?"

So they had, a clumsy mating dance of the female of the species, full of suspicion and raw passion. They hadn't talked much during it, their voices crushed or carried away by the thumping bass of the Glamour Pussies from the stage. But then they did have a conversation, carried through the language of shaded eyes and pursed lips. No words, but intent nonetheless.

Before they fell asleep together, arms wrapped in a Gordian knot of spent passion, she'd spoken, words laced with Spanish moss and green drinks on the verandah.

"I think I'll like it here."

* * * *

A day, maybe two. The Peterson file was open but bare of any work. Every hour it seemed, something new surfaced, some detail of that night. The glow of her skin, pale — almost translucent — but lit from within by some kind of raw light, pure energy. The ferocity of her love-making, as if she'd been trying to crawl inside Ellie. The throbbing of the bruise on her neck, the way her belle had smiled and licked at the chafe gently, apologetically.

"So, who is she?" Jennifer said, poking her bob-haired head around the corner.

Ellie blushed, warmth spreading down her neck.

"Just someone I met."

"Oh! Just someone or a special someone?"

Her eyes danced with excitement at seeing this side of Ellie.

"Special, I think," Ellie said. "I hope."

"You haven't heard from her?"

Concern this time, maybe that sweet, innocent Ellie had been waylaid by the dyke version of a "wham-bam-thank-you m'am"

The thought had never occurred to Ellie. Hadn't heard from her? Had it really been days? No calls. No flowers. No letters. No U-Haul (to play to the old joke). Nothing. Yet there wasn't fear in that, wasn't that normal stomach-dropping shame of actually hoping for something good to happen. None of that. Just the soft, warm glow in her belly — the desire, the affection, remaining — undiluted, still there.

"Not really," Ellie said, her voice sounding lost, as if from far away.

"Oh, Ellie!" Jennifer said, moving around the corner to put a warm hand on Ellie's. "Don't take it too hard."

"I won't, I promise," she said, with mock sincerity, just to make the other woman go away. She wanted to be alone with the thoughts she was having, the warm swell of emotions. No, she hadn't heard from her. No, she didn't know where she was. But then it also seemed, somehow, like she'd never left.

* * * *

Getting up the next morning, a name: Samantha. The revelation was a bolt, a brilliant stroke through her, making Ellie's body respond. A smile. Samantha. Yes, perfect, a bell-ringing tone of truth. Her name was Samantha. Brushing her teeth, she remembered the color of her eyes: gray, like burnished steel.

Pulling on her pantyhose, she remembered her breath: sweet, a lingering touch of the beers they'd shared. She remembered the way it was hot on her neck after their first, consuming kiss. A slow pant that warmed Ellie's already burning skin. Sweet…

Driving to work, she knew that Samantha of the sweet breath had been slightly shorter, not enough to crane the neck, but enough to put the hesitant Ellie at ease.

Arriving — chocolate.

Little Samantha with the sweet breath had asked if she'd had some. Ellie, whose face exploded if she had even a cup of coffee, had to disappoint.

But Samantha, sweet Samantha, had just smiled and said that she'd get her own later. Then, the kiss.

An hour later, Peterson's file opened and ignored, she remembered her feet as they slept together, the way she'd kicked, like a cat in a dream of chasing mice, her rough nails scratching Ellie's tender ankles, drawing her out of her dream.

More, too much more. Panting with the cascade, Ellie locked herself in the bathroom for an hour, letting her body recall what her mind couldn't comprehend. She knew she was risking embarrassment, but didn't care — what was coming … came.

Only Jennifer seemed to notice.

She stopped by as Ellie was packing to leave. Concern darkened her face.

"I just don't want you to get hurt," she'd said, then repeated the offer that Ellie should call if she needed to.

Ellie agreed, again just to get away, to get back to her memory of that one night.

"Ah will," she said, hearing the honey and Savannah tones slip out from between her lips: "Ah will, sweetie. Ah will."

✳ ✳ ✳ ✳

Key in the lock. Blues were her favorite music. Bathroom, water splashed on her face. She loved dark nights, no moon. Sunlight was alien, distant. Shoes off, dress thrown onto the floor. Walking the streets of New Orleans long before they could even be called streets. Women in hoop skirts, carrying umbrellas, elegant Creoles with their sing-song voices. Boys running by, chasing a wayward, and terrified, chicken.

The rest of it came off, naked and under the covers, shivering as if from a cold, a fever. Yellow fever, people dying all around her.

Healthy, she'd taken to theatrical symptoms to ward off suspicion, having to be careful about who she chose, not wanting to inherit the illness.

Covers over her head, body quaking. World War II, starched clothing and chafing nylons. Many soldiers, in and out; many women, lurking around Charleston, lost and hungry. She, just hungry. Much confusion, and in that an easy way of living.

She missed wars. Because she could only be with women, she still missed the chaos, the frantic sloppiness of unrest. Peace was meticulous, peace was pedantic. People in peace had nothing better than to miss people, look for them, try and track them down.

Too much, a torrent, a heavy rain of images. Many faces, many times, many eyes looking at her with amused relief, many shoes on many feet, many nights with many women. Those eyes, always the same reflection, always the same attitude, always the same.

Ellie, while there was an Ellie, realized the sameness, saw it with a shocking knowledge. Always the same attitude, because no matter whose eyes they all housed Samantha and she was looking in a mirror.

I love you, Ellie thought as it became too much, as she drowned under the heavy sea of Samantha's many years — loving her, caring for her, till the end.

✳ ✳ ✳ ✳

Later that night, the moon bright and new, she awoke, the storm having passed. Clarity. Nothing but today, nothing but her body under the sheets. Stiff, muscles quivering from strain and tension, she got up, looking at herself in the full-length mirror. The bruise was fading, as it always did, the stigmata of waking, the sign of another month.

One more month before blood on the sheets again. Slowly, getting used to new muscles, new bones, new tendons, her senses, Samantha got dressed.

127

I love you, too, Ellie, Samantha thought, looking at her face one last time in the mirror, car keys flashing silver in her right hand, *at least as much as I love myself.*

Then, she smiled and went out.

EXCERPT FROM THE NOVEL *BRUSHES*

due out from Parisian Phoenix Kink in Spring 2025

Chapter Six: Diego

A button? Because of a button on his uniform — no, not just a button. Less than a button. Because of a button that should have been on his uniform, Louis had crooked a plump finger, hooking him with authority and seniority into the passageway. Then with a sneer, then a frown, then a bullying roar he had taken an average, ordinary day of punching tickets on the LeHavre line away from Diego, replacing it with a sour bellyache and an early evening of sitting on the dirty cement of a loading dock, staring out at a fat, rosy sun going down through tangles of phone and power lines, then finally setting behind rows of cheap apartments. And drinking.

One sip, he told himself as he hung his uniform up in his locker. One sip, he told himself when he brushed his own fingers — tough and straight and honest working — over the missing button. One sip, he told himself walking out the door, waving to the other conductors, nodding to a few greasy engineers, and then around the corner and back into the yards, to sit in his favorite forgotten corner of the maintenance bays, to stare at night arriving along with a few rumbling expresses and a pair of cooler, calmer local trains.

Louis, though, made him think of Uncle Santos' house. Thick plaster walls; tiny paintings of even tinier Basque villages; decanters of thick, sweet liquors; and a brass serving tray. Sitting on filthy cement in his street clothes, he toasted the twists and vortices of memory, the cheap bourbon burning his throat; the way a portly supervisor complaining about a missing button could lead him to sitting, drinking, seeing a brass serving tray in a distant uncle's house in Northern Spain — and then drinking more while thinking of Elena.

That color. Not just blond, not almost gold. Elena's hair had been the color of that finely polished metal. An assistant teacher at their small local school, she'd been only two years older but a world apart. An ideal carrying books and papers, a dream pointing to distant lands on a map, a fantasy correcting his division in red pen.

Ever since she'd arrived with those books and papers, spending days teaching the class where India was, and where to put an extra six in a math problem, she'd been supple and heated in his mind — especially late at night, after he was sure his brother was asleep. In a classroom after the other students had gone home, when she was bathing somewhere he could peek, she would welcome him inside her house, wherever that was, after he'd gotten caught in a pounding, blustering rainstorm. Too young to have his own fantasies, he'd borrowed from the crackling pages of the old magazines hidden under his bed, closing his eyes and superimposing her brass-haloed head over the black and white images, putting her imagined body into various positions.

No idea what would happen when she unbuttoned her stiff, starched blouse in that cool and dark school, or stood up from that pool or pond or stream or tub with water streaming down her thighs, or after she slipped his arms from the heavy sleeves of his sopping sweater and his hand accidentally brushed the plushness of a breast. The magazines were frustratingly chaste, tantalizing rather than informing him of the mysteries beneath the models' antique undergarments.

After, he'd sleep — hand sticky, sheet sticky, blanket sticky — wishing before other dreams came that she'd show him what the magazines teased, give him one of their wicked, inviting grins.

Elena. Yeah, Elena. One sip, then another, the cement hard and inflexible under his ass. Two sips, then three. The memory just as hard and abrasive as the loading dock. A new twist, a new turn. And, just as Uncle Santos' brass serving tray lead to Elena, Elena eventually swung around to three sips, then four.

Another night, after dinner, with his own books and papers, trying to find Argentina, trying to find out how many times twelve fit into one hundred twenty-nine, all while his brother sat at the other desk in their room, doing what he always did: pad of paper, pencil in one pudgy hand, lines and curves, sweeps and rapid scratches of shading, tight concentrations of detail, hazy generalized backgrounds. But that one night, after that one dinner, the dark eyes were more focused than usual, one arm hooked around the pad, keeping the specifics of those lines, those curves, those sweeps and rapid scratches hidden.

Four sips. Then Diego took the bottle from his lips, rubbed a dirty thumb across the label. The lettering was elegant, fluid. Some work had gone into the design. He might not have had his brother's talent, but he still could recognize a skilled hand when he saw it.

Just like he'd seen it when Escobar had gone to bed, and Diego had stolen a look at what his brother had been feverishly working on. Too young to really appreciate it, at least not with an adult's vocabulary or cultivated sensibilities, he'd been struck dumb and still at what he saw on the pad. It was lovely, haunting, sensual, and revealing. It had smoothness of form, suppleness of texture. That was how it was haunting. It was full and rich, luxurious in its shading, solid in its realism. That was its sensuality.

And revealing. Yes, revealing. A naked woman, with nothing hidden, all her mysteries for the world — and the artist — to see. All the folds, the creases, the puckers, and the pelt of hair. But without being coarse or crude.

And revealing. It was a sketch of Elena.

Four sips, and Diego put the cap back on the bottle and returned the bottle to his coat pocket. Twists and turns. Things revealed that had only been a mystery before. A month ago he would have swallowed the whole bottle, thrown the empty glass at the gleaming tracks, and stumbled off to his little apartment to pass out on dirty sheets.

That was before. Now, Diego had somewhere to go, something to do, find a gallery opening, and become a famous artist.

* * * *

Things had changed, but he still had to go back to his place. It was cold in the winter and steaming in the summer, the stereo in the little café underneath made his dishes and cups dance and jingle when it was played too loud, which was most of the time, and the design of his kitchen, bathroom, living room, and bedroom was a jumble of odd-sized steps and crooked walls. He'd been there for five years and never once thought about moving.

It wasn't that he dreamed of better, or that he'd grown too accustomed to sweating, shivering, listening to thumping bass, or stumbling from room to room, because after five long years, he hadn't.

Laying down in his too-soft bed, hands knitted behind his head, staring up at peeling paint on the sagging ceiling, he often thought about other twists and turns, a different sperm, a different egg, been born Escobar instead of Diego.

Nice? Definitely. To have a car instead of sore feet and a bus pass. Relaxing? Absolutely. To never have to worry about money, to be able to buy anything — *anything* — without a second thought. Exciting? Assuredly. Flashes of cameras, fawning interviewers asking how it is to be a success, models and actresses demanding your attention. Pleasurable? Positively. To see your handiwork hanging on so many very famous walls, on the covers of so many magazines.

At first, he'd only managed to slip into restless sleep after swallowing bitter denial, rocking himself to sleep with sour fantasies. His brother was too foolish to buy a really good car, or that the insurance premiums were insanely high, or even with chrome and plush leather, the car and its passengers would still have to sit and fume in constant, strangling traffic. That the taxman would take every other dollar, that bookkeepers clattering with devious calculators would take nibbles and then monstrous bites of his fortune, that for each thousand he made the cost of even the simplest thing would rise to meet and then surpass it — hundred-franc cheeses, thousand-franc glasses of red, million-franc vacations, when the best of holidays was sitting in the afternoon sun sipping excellent cheap wine and sampling robust and inexpensive *fromage*. That for each dazzle of a camera, for every sycophantic question, there was a little man in a trench coat following him down the street, pushing lenses into his tiniest, tightest, most private of private indulgences and screaming them in headlines on every tabloid from London to Tokyo. That for every thunderstorm of applause, every medal, every ribbon, there was the itch in the back of the skull, the fast-drumming heartbeat that the next might be the one received with frowns, shown with shaken heads rather than nods, or that one day another will walk into the spotlight and the critics and buyers will say to the mentioning of your name 'who' instead of 'genius!'

Diego used to think all that, examining his sagging present, and drift to sleep relishing in the purity of his simple life, disparaging the maintenance of fine cars, scorning the weight of too much money, shocked by the prying eyes, or dismissing the precarious pedestal of fame. No, it was better, much better, to sip from the noble bottle of being a common man, loving the purity of an honest job, and sampling the earthly cheeses of life. He might be poor, but he was the salt of the earth, with a pride Escobar never could afford, and that Diego would never, ever sell.

But then something had happened, a night that had changed it all. Not that Diego had changed in the way he viewed his jumbled apartment, his miniscule paycheck, or anything else about his unpretentious life. Instead, it had changed the way he felt when sleep washed over him, still gazing up at the sagging ceiling of his apartment. No bitterness, not any more. If anything, he looked at his life with a true and genuine smile, and his brother with true and honest pity.

After all, Diego had found a way to have everything his brother had, and more, without any of the weights of luxury, fame, money, or exposure.

It was good. Very good indeed.

II

"Aren't you...?"

He'd been in a bookstore. Why he was in a bookstore, he couldn't remember. Maybe it'd been raining outside and the stacks had been a place to dry off, wait for the drops to stop falling. Maybe he'd stopped in to flick through magazines he couldn't afford.

Whatever the reason, he was in a bookstore, a newly opened bookstore. A young man, a student, snot-nosed kid, bright button eyes under coal-black hair, pale face over fashionable sweater, portfolio under one arm, had asked him that.

Suspicion and heart-fluttering paranoia had made Diego stammer something negative.

"No." "Not me." "I don't know what you mean."

Something like that. Whatever he'd sputtered, the student's young face sagged into middle-age from disappointment and he'd turned to fade back into the shelves of books.

Who had he thought Diego was? A criminal flashed on the late night news? The newsreader's tone serious and heavy while telling the horrible story of this rogue who stole from the rich and kept it?

Or possibly his face was from a larger screen, a set of invading features from America, the newest rugged star from the plains of cowboys and Indians. Did he share the slope of a nose, the penetrating stare, the perfect coif of a new Brando, an original Victor Mature, a fresh John Wayne?

The question nagged at him, a persistent itch of thought, as he wandered through the brightly lit modern space from mysteries to romance, from science to the newsstand. Among the brightly, glossy, stylish cover models, he looked around but didn't really see any of their smooth faces. But then one cover caught his eye and he'd known whom the student had mistook him for.

The likeness wasn't good, but it was still there. A family nose, family eyes, family hair. Sure, Diego was five years older than his brother, but there were similarities in features nonetheless.

"Fucker," Diego had muttered, too loudly as one of the girls behind the counter, clicking keys on the register, had looked up with sour disapproval on her own bright, glossy, cover model face.

He'd wanted to rip *Art News* in half, reducing his brother's face to shreds, crushing his success down to litter, ruining his headline to garbage. Holding the magazine, the stiff paper of the cover cutting into his fingers and palms, though, he'd stopped. In part because he couldn't pay for it, but also because he'd realized that, yes, the student hadn't seen Diego, the railway conductor, but rather Escobar, the painter.

He'd stayed in that bookstore, drifting from one end of the building to the other, from music to politics, from history to games, but mostly around the section marked "Art," in simple sans serif letters. He even stood for almost half an hour with one of his brother's books in his hands, the base of the heavy spine pressing into his waist, turning page after page of masterpieces, hoping that another fresh-faced student, maybe even a bright, glossy, cover model aficionado would wander by and make the same mistake.

But none did.

* * * *

"Excuse me, but aren't you...?"

Standing, he'd craned forward slightly to show concentration. He hadn't turned around at the voice. Just as he'd rehearsed in his mind. Both he and the owner of the voice were in a tiny gallery in a less-than-trendy, less-than-important little neighborhood too close to a third-rate art college, too far from the first-rate one.

On two of the walls were a series of tiny lithographs, black and white frozen moments of classic — and very extinct — street life: men in top hats and cravats, women in blooming skirts and bonnets. In the back, a scarred and battered table with a visitor's book open only to its first page, the names written only halfway down, and a bottle of very *ordinaire* vintage, a topple of glasses scavenged no doubt from a local café, a wedge of cheap cheese and a thickly sliced baguette that could very easily have been a day old. It was perfect. He couldn't have hoped for anything better.

"I'm sorry," he said after a carefully stretched minute, turning away from the idealized man, the perfect woman, to become who he wasn't to speak to someone not of dreams, but instead, just of the moment. "I was lost in this work."

"You were?" she said, eyes large, mouth bright with a smile. "That's great."

"It shows promise," he said, looking critically at the young woman, studying her shades, lines, contours, shape, and form.

Short but not too short. Full cheeks that got even fuller, redder, plumper when she smiled, which was what she was doing. Blue eyes, naturally bright and clear. Sparkles there, amazement and pleasure.

"Honestly?"

Black dress, dyed also, though less obviously than her hair, not showing much of her body, but from what he could deduce, it was full and rich and bountiful. Thick thighs, gentle round belly, full pendulous breasts, round little ass.

"Honestly," he said about her promise, sincere in his lie.

He was amazed he wasn't more nervous, it being his first time, or his brother's first time or his first time as his brother. But he wasn't. What was the worst that could happen? A slap? A scream? But a slap to whose face? A scream about whose inappropriateness?

"That means a lot coming from you," she said, eyes even brighter, little goddess body shifting deliciously as she rocked back and forth on her heels in nervousness. "It really does."

Shrugging, he gave her a simple grin. He didn't have much to go with, his brother being shy, preferring his studio to the outside world. But by a week or so after that time in the bookstore, the first time he realized how much his brother and he had in common, at least with the position of noses, mouths, eyebrows, and eyes. He'd managed to put together a pretty effective costume based on his own knowledge of Escobar and a few paparazzi shots. Later, he'd refined his performance down to the smallest possible detail.

Still later, things had changed even more. Not in his costume or his acting, but the point of his performance: the kind of applause he'd asked for, and received from, various young and nubile artists.

But that was months after that first gallery, that first girl.

"I try to be true in all things. In art and in my life. Your work has true potential, as do you." Thinking that maybe he'd pushed it too far, he turned back to the lithographs. "I see the possibility of great work here."

"I still can't believe... Well, you're you and you're saying that."

Looking back to her, he saw dimples and full cheeks get even fuller.

"I am. You are a beautiful woman who does beautiful things."

Not a lie, not really, just the truth stretched, pulled out of shape. It wasn't that she wasn't pretty, which she was, or that her artwork didn't have merit, because to his fairly untrained eye it seemed to be good enough, but it wasn't Escobar who'd said it.

Where to go from there was another matter. Embarrassment, not for his costume or performance, reddened his cheeks and heated his chest. Research, rehearsal. When it came to truly exploiting the familial resemblance, he hadn't planned that detail, the finishing touch.

Ideas came and went: too rough, too smooth, too quick, too slow. Escobar wouldn't suggest a drink somewhere. Escobar wouldn't just stroke her hair. Escobar wouldn't give her a pinch. Escobar...

He'd no idea how his brother acted with a girl. He'd been there, of course, when his brother had begun seeing Constance, but as always, Escobar seemed more interested in his sketches and studies than sharing with his brother what they did together. Diego, frightened of his brother's possible genius at love as well, certainly hadn't asked Escobar about it. Even when Escobar married Constance, there hadn't been a chance to study him, her pure beauty having turned Diego's stomach bitter and he'd spent the day in a haze of too-much wine.

Diego knew what to do with a woman. The older, rougher, brother knew. He just didn't know how to translate his experience into his disguise as his brother.

Maybe that was it: an offer to pose, a suggestion to model? No, not enough time, and besides, where would he take her?

His failure to plan the final seduction for this initial impersonation, had made him ball his cleaned and buffed (for the night) fingers into fists. Fuck this. Fuck Escobar. Fuck his big house, his big car, his face in magazines, his artwork on walls. Fuck it all.

"This really means a lot to me," she'd repeated.

This time, her hand was on his arm, fingers warm even through the thickness of his best coat. Looking down at her face, into her liquid eyes, he saw heat there, steam there, burning there, melting there, hot there.

"If there's any way I can thank you..."

The answer made him smile, bloomed his hands from a pair of fists into one hand spread across the small of her back, the other on her own arm. The answer relaxed him, the question of 'where to go from here' vanishing with it. Let her come to him.

Which is what he did, that first time, in that first gallery, still getting used to his costume as his brother. They chatted a bit more, Diego falling comfortably into his performance as the kind, successful, passionate artist. The chatting led to more cheap wine, the cheap wine led to his hand on her thigh, his hand on her thigh led to her leaning in close, her leaning in close led to their first kiss, their first kiss lasted for a long time — a moment of her soft moans and his deeper, harder ones — and finally led to the gallery owner telling them he had to close up.

It all led to a late night in a very dark city. A new question emerged as they walked away from the now-dark space. Where to from here? His wallet was dry and dusty, a little money and a credit card he couldn't use. Escobar the great, Escobar the famous wouldn't have her pick up the tab for a room, nor would he stumble back to her no doubt tiny apartment somewhere.

The wine had helped. His hands didn't return to stressed clutches of fingers. This last question was merely a technical detail, a reservation perhaps in a nearby hotel, traveling into town as an excuse, as opposed to a larger, more difficult problem of how to get even close to that planned room, that final element in the seduction. If not that first time, then definitely later.

He'd almost laughed. Almost.

He had smiled, though, when she'd held him tight, jerked him towards the tall, dark, narrow yawn of an alleyway, mumbling as she did, "Come here. I know you have a wife and all, but I have to do this. Just a taste, you know? Hope you don't mind. I really want to do this. Really."

In that soft darkness, her lips on his, then a soft feminine hand touched his tight, throbbing thigh. Then... well, then a soft feminine hand between his thighs, gripping then massaging him into dizzying hardness, head-spinning firmness. Just when he was going to grab her, turn her, and lift those heavy skirts of hers, she stopped, breaking her grip and lifting her lips from his.

The power of fame, he remembered thinking, the clarity of the thought like a monster church bell in his head, rising above the bubbling, fuming, bellowing roar of his erection and its demand for release.

In that alley, in a darkness filled only with ghostly trash bins and pale veins of drain pipes, she carefully crouched down and began working on his fly. That almost brought his orgasm to its peak, just the thought, the concept, the idea of it: that she would get down on her knees in an alley for him, for Escobar, of course — but right then and thinking about it afterward, it didn't matter. What did was that she was on her knees, in that alley, and working on his fly.

Then, it wasn't work, far from it. Then, it was those plump lips of hers on him, beginning with a kiss, then a lick, then a swallow, then all of that up and down and back and forth, followed by her tight grip on his shaft.

It wasn't perfect. In fact, in the great scheme of a woman's lips on his dick, it wasn't even good. Her teeth grazed the so-sensitive head of his cock a few too many times. The teeth of his fly felt like they were going to saw through the thick shaft. She didn't put enough pressure in her actual sucking, too much saliva making sensation distant and too slippery.

But it was still good, great, fantastic, wonderful.

Because she was on her knees, in an alley, and she was sucking his cock. That, more than her actual actions, was what boiled him, steamed him, tensed his back, and make him thrust back and forth in concert with her lips and hands and throat. He felt it start, and not just start but begin too strong, too demanding, too powerful to try and push aside, to distract himself away from it, to prolong.

Yelling, bellowing, roaring, he came very hard, very fast. Dizzy when it ebbed, he put his hand onto cold brick to steady himself. Panting, chest straining as it tried to get enough air, he felt even his braced legs turn to meaty jelly. A few more deep, soothing breaths returned his balance.

"Was it good?" she asked, rising to her feet in front of him, her wicked grin gleaming even in the dimness of the alley.

Licking her lips, she ran her own quivering hand down his chest, a gesture that immediately made him think about doing it again, and again, and again.

But it was late, she was a young art student, and he was not Escobar. There would be other times, definitely. He knew that. Not with this girl, that first conquest, but with new ones. Now it was time to smile, to pat her head, to wish her the best, and to move on.

But first... What would Escobar do? What would his brother do?

It was easy, the easiest answer of that night, the comfort of it warm and welcoming around him. His brother was the role he was born to play.

"You are a beautiful woman," he said to her, lifting her chin and looking into her wet, deep eyes. "A woman who does beautiful things."

III

"So much for fame and fortune getting you a good room. I must apologize. This was the best they had available."

"Oh, I don't mind. It's kind of charming in its own way."

A narrow girl, a vertical woman: all leg and tight muscles, thin breasts and strong lines of cheekbones. Black jeans and a similarly charcoal-shaded silk blouse, parting here and there to reveal a thin strap that could very well lead to an elegant bra. She tried to costume her aristocracy, put her in the role of a proletarian artist, but her genetic precision betrayed her.

It was a bonus, not that he would have passed on the opportunity if her parents had been schoolteachers, grocery store managers, clerks, or even railway conductors. She was a woman, a struggling artist hungry for fame, and he was someone who had it. Or so she thought.

"You are too kind. Another trait one so rarely finds in the world of paint and canvas. Promise me you will never lose that," Diego said, closing the door behind him.

The night had been warm, touching hot, and so she had no coat he could gallantly offer to take from her.

"Can I order you something to drink?" he asked, hand on the old phone by the bed.

"That would be nice, but it's not really important," she said, eyes gleaming bright. Tall and thin, narrow and upright, those eyes and the way she stood said that while her genes might be old and noble, tonight she was just a giggling girl. "I still can't believe I met you."

"I could very easily say the same," Diego said. It was at least six months after that first clumsy alley. He'd been practicing. "But let me assure you, I'm just a man, like many others."

"Oh, no, you're not! I mean, goodness, just your work on the *Pieces of Infinite* alone... is just incredible. I saw them in the Prado last summer when I was down there with my parents. All I could do was just goggle at them. *Zero Point Zero* is my favorite, though they all are, really, but that one with the streaks of rose, the tiny bits of gold leaf, the perfect placement of the two black triangles. I mean... Shit, listen to me. I can't talk about them, but they are all just so damned perfect. I'm sorry. I must sound like a complete idiot."

He laughed, almost like a small cough.

"Nonsense. Not at all. I know what you mean. I really do. I feel the same way about Monet. It was fun to do, but... Well, it's just paint and canvas, you know? Just art."

"Oh, no," she said, her emerald eyes bright in the poorly lit room. "No, no — I'm sorry, but I don't think that's what it is at all. I mean, with me, that's all it is. But you... My God, what you do with it is so much more than that. When I saw your *Perfect Glow* in the Tate, I... It was the best thing I'd ever seen. I mean that. It is just so powerful, and perfect, and elegant, and... I have it in my apartment, you know. A poster of it, I mean. Sometimes I just sit and stare at it. The way the colors, the composition... And here you are. I still can't believe it. I really can't."

His face was hot. The room was close, confining.

"Please, stop. I eat, breathe, and even shit. I'm no better than anyone else, not really."

"I don't believe that. What you do... It's just too wonderful. I think sometimes I might be able to do one or two good paintings, enough to get me some kind of attention, but that's all. I know I don't have it and that's okay. You, though, you have the magic. You really do. I wish I could show you how stunning I think your work is, how much it's affected me, changed me. I just want to say... I just want to say 'thank you,' Escobar. Thank you for your work. Thank you so much."

She sniffled once, then twice. Stretching out a long, thin arm, she pulled a tissue from a marred leather box sitting on a side table. Ladylike — a betraying, refined gesture — she dabbed at her suddenly pink nose.

"I'm sorry, I-I... It's just..."

"Oh, stop it," he said. He reached down, hooked his hands where her narrow arms flowed into her streamlined chest, and pulled her to her feet. "Look... I'm not some kind of saint, okay? Just a guy, just a man."

"N-no," she said. "I know that. I do. Sorry."

"It's okay," he said, the room feeling like a sauna. Stepping back from her, he shook off his coat, tossing it at a chair after it slid from his shoulders. "It is. I'm just a man. I'm not perfect."

"Okay," she said, looking suddenly very small and rather fragile. "I-I understand. It's just..."

She shook her head.

"It's what?" he asked, the temperature inside himself knocking up a few more degrees. "That I'm famous? That's bullshit. You know that. It's all bullshit. I could have been a fucking cab driver, punch tickets on a train or something. I was just fucking lucky. Just because I paint fucking pictures doesn't mean I'm any better than any other asshole. Fuck, you think I got you up here to talk about painting?"

Shaking her head, she squeaked out a tiny noise of negativity.

"No, Monsieur Escobar." she finally said, voice soft and small.

He touched her breast. No, not accurate. Not the scene and not the way he was feeling, the way he acted. Better: he grabbed her tit. Small, his hand cupped the entire rise of it, the kernel of nipple poking at his palm. He kneaded, hard and quick, feeling blouse and bra and soft skin slide against each other.

"This is why I brought you up here, okay? You got that? You understand? I want to fuck you. That's all. Not to talk about my fucking painting or how fucking great I am. You made my dick hard, that's all."

Nodding her head, she gasped out a miniscule sound of agreement.

"Okay," she said, her tone supple and passive.

It made his face burn. Even though she'd already begun to work free the first button on her blouse, he pushed her fingers away.

"You're too fucking slow," he said, the room very tight, way too small, his voice way too loud.

The next and then the next and the next, resisting with each one to just yank it off, bounce buttons off the too-near walls. Her bra was white and simple, everyday wear. No lace, no satin. Between the pearl-colored straps, her chest was smooth, the slow rises of her breasts below the cups revealing that she bought a size too big. The insecurity made her seem even smaller, more delicate, more fragile.

Fingers sliding along her shoulders, then under those straps, he slipped them free. Tight and small, the arrangement paused then dropped down, a loose belt of cotton and satin around her narrow waist.

She was whimpering. Those shoulders rose, her hands climbed but then slowed, finally stopping short before she could cover herself — a gesture agreeing with his hands, his eyes, his thundering heart, the persistent erection in his suddenly confining pants.

No, an agreement not with him, and that burned him even more. The bra came off with an assurance that surprised him, the hooks usually far more cryptic and confusing. It went somewhere behind him, tossed with strength but its trajectory encouraged by its near weightlessness.

Hard was not an accurate way to describe her nipples. This was the first time he'd seen a body like hers, peaked and firm, breasts of pure alabaster, a form from classical sculpture. Grecian, Roman, but fresh and new, just cut from young marble with none of the rough soil or cracks of history. The tips of her breasts were bright rosy swells of sweet skin, less nipple and more large, puffy areola.

Exotic, unusual. For a time, he could only stare. The room was quiet, not even the sounds of midnight Paris coming through to him. Her breathing, though, was loud: a steady, deep in, slow out of air.

The anger was gone, the sight of her draining it away. Its only legacy was his rigid cock, originally raised in fury but now determined at the sight of her.

Bending down, he brushed his lips across the hot, smooth swell of one areola, a controlled movement painfully stately with restraint. Not just turning the graze into a kiss and then a firm suck was a form of torture, directed completely towards his erection.

She responded, even if he held back. With the first touch of lips to skin, her breathing went from steady in, slow out to a gasping intake, a sigh of exhalation. Hands previously at her side rose to the sides of his head, firmly grasping his ears, and with a determined pull, she did what he held back — pressed his mouth completely to her puffy nipple.

His suck was firm, passionate, as was her response, guttural sounds from deep down within, then knees sagging, her descent pulling the silken skin from his mouth with a soft, wet sound.

Gasping, she carefully regained her footing. Back of a hand to her forehead, she giggled and sighed. He reached down to her hand and pulled her even further upright with a single word.

"Bed."

She responded with her own solitary one: "okay."

On the way, she shed the rest of what few items of clothing remained: a trotting strip revealing more and more lithe skin. Finally, standing on one side of the bed, she was naked and glowing, a tender rose of excitement. As she moved, falling in a cascade of arms and legs to lay on the bedspread, he caught sight of the moistness painting the insides of her thighs and felt his already hammering heart fist-hard in his chest.

His own clothes fell away and he was suddenly aware and frustrated by the number of zippers, belts, buttons, and elastic he had to deal with. But soon enough, he'd joined her in bareness.

And soon enough he'd joined her on the bed. Arms, legs, skin, heat, wet, hard, tongue, nipples, breasts, cheeks... A cascade of one to another to another to another, all to a melody of equal and mutual deep noises.

Then he was on top of her, then inside of her. Her heat and wetness were an electric bolt from his erection through his body to somewhere between his eyes. Fighting the need to shove himself up and over into a bolt of orgasm, he struggled to focus on something, anything, but what he was actually doing. Pushing and pumping, his attention darted to a painting hanging over the bed, a street scene of Paris, somewhere around the turn of the century. He didn't know the technique, but he did see its commonness, its cheapness, its averageness. It was just one of a million, all of them perfectly the same.

Then, she bent with athletic, blind passion, her eyes out of focus, her face shimmering with sweat, to lock her lips around his nipple. She may have used her teeth, might have actually bit him in her blind drive, but he never knew because what focus he had was gone and he found himself screaming and groaning in a whole body-shake orgasm.

And down, a puppet with its wires cut, to fall onto her heaving belly, forehead grasping the plushness of breast. Time elongated, became a moment of unknown duration, only broken when she started to play with his dark curls.

"That was wonderful," she said in a tender voice.

Responding with a kiss to a nipple, he smiled up at her. "Mutual, darling."

"I still can't believe..." she began, face beaming down at him. "That it was with you... Escobar."

That wasn't the one that changed it all. That wasn't the one that moved his whole world around. But, still, her reminder of what he was — just a cheap thing, just one of a million, and not a masterpiece — was an ice pick, a short, sharp shock that brought him up and out of a near-dozing bliss and to his feet, caused him to say "Yeah, whatever," and fish for his clothes, to put them on, and then get out of that small hotel room as fast as he could, slamming the door behind him.

IV

Months later, he was getting ready to go out again. Once again, he assembled his studied impersonation, moving his hair this way and that until it came close to the picture of his brother he'd taped to his bathroom mirror. He carefully trimmed, shaved, and primped himself until both faces, one real, one a copy, were as close as he could make them.

Then came the clothes. Expensive, but when one is creating something, one should use the right materials. He wondered, sliding his arms into the coat, if that was how his brother felt, picking and choosing his paints and canvas, his brushes and paper. A few months ago, the question would have made Diego punch his bed, maybe even the wall, in rage. A twist of fate, one sperm, one egg different, and he and not his brother would have been carefully selecting just the right pigment, the perfect weight of parchment that could — no, *would* — hang on a famous wall someplace. The great, the famous, the talented, the celebrated Escobar... and his unknown, distant, forgotten brother.

But that was before that one night and the woman who changed it.

Thinking of her brought an echo, a wave of *déjà vu.* Another night, another ritual of preparation turning one brother into another with a different kind of brush, working on the flesh and blood canvas of his own face. That night, though, his plans had been very different.

A hotel? Absolutely. Reservations, in fact, made for a moderately expensive one. He wished his paycheck could afford a better one, to help the illusion, but he'd gotten very good at all kinds of explanations.

"Only thing in the area" was his favorite. Research? Accomplished. Even though Escobar had avoided much of the spotlight he'd stepped into, its penetrating glare was enough for Diego to put together a convincing depiction.

Goal? Into the mirror he'd leered, changing his portrait of a middle-aged man from an artist of incredible ability and noble bearing to a beast out for one thing.

He'd gone out with that in mind. Theft via impersonation might have been how he'd begun, to have a taste of what his brother no doubt feasted on every night, but that's not how it had progressed. Instead of seduction, he'd gone out that night — the night when it had all changed — to, yes, enjoy sticking his dick in some poor art student's hungry cunt, but more to stick it to his brother.

143

More exactly: his brother's reputation.

* * * *

"Aren't you...?"

He'd been standing there, looking intently at her work for what had seemed like hours, but was probably just a few minutes, his time sense multiplied by impatience.

"Why, yes. Yes, I am — if you mean someone looking at your art."

Carefully refined, it was a line practiced many times in front of the mirror. Designed wit, perfected charm.

A little gallery near the college, just like a dozen or so before. No surprises there: a wooden-walled box, window in front, table with wine and cheese in the back. Arriving late, as he'd always done, to avoid the crowd, and with it, too many eyes.

"Do you... do you like them?" She'd asked, just as others had.

A question warbling with hope. That little student, the young artist, wanting more than anything for the great artist to look down from his genius, his wealth, his fame, to pat her on the head and say that she, too, could join him on the covers of magazines, to maybe walk into a life like his.

"Not all of them, no," he said, also meticulously honed, another thoroughly crafted performance. To say he liked them all would be unrealistic, too smarmy. To say that some of them had potential implied an honest standard. "But some show promise."

"T-thank you," she'd stammered, like they all had stammered, paralyzed by his lights.

"No," he'd said, grinning with the appearance of warmth. "Thank *you*. This one, particularly, shows serious promise."

"The *Arc de Triomphe*?" she'd said in a low, hushed voice. The obvious stated, she'd blushed, a petaled glow rising to her cheeks.

"Yes."

Turning away from her, he pretended to study it. The play was for him to praise one work, say that it was as good as anything he'd done — that Escobar had done — at her age. To say she had potential. From there, he would walk her around the gallery, nodding at some, shaking his head at others, all the time sliding intimacy between his lines, hints, and suggestions that she was special not just because of her talent, but also her beauty, her passion, her sensuality.

From there... from there, to an alley in some cases, to the hotel in others.

An hour, or two, or three, or perhaps even waking in the morning to tangled legs, tangled sheets.

Alley, hotel, or the morning after, all to end the same way. Praise for the artist, adoration for Escobar, his brother, all to end the same way, a new line practiced in front of his mirror: "That was nice enough. But you understand that a man of my position has to be careful of the company he keeps."

And the like, and more of the like, and still more of the like, until she was in tears, great heaving sobs of disappointment and shame.

Pleasure for Diego from a night with a young and eager woman. A reputation shadowed, rumors whispered, for Escobar. Pleasure, as well, for Diego, because of those shades across his brother, the rumors that would be whispered.

Business as usual. Fun as usual. But not that night.

That night he looked at two things.

The first was the sketch she'd made of the *Triomphe*.

Art had been Escobar's land, Diego's brother's territory, surrendered to him with bitterness and resentment after his first acknowledgment of talent. But that wasn't to say that the elder brother didn't know "good" when he saw it. Before he'd watched Escobar sail off into fame and success, Diego had even thought about going in that direction himself. But, as said, and as even more deeply felt, that was gone. But also said, also felt, he still had a connection to it.

He'd lied to her, not just about being his brother, or his reasons for being at her showing. There was another sin, one of not quite omission, but rather one of degree. The sketch wasn't just good, it was incredible. With only a few carefully chosen lines, a few darkened patches, she'd captured not just the appearance, but also the power and importance of the *Arc de Triomphe*. It had weight, it had texture, it had dimension — and for including all of that in a small square of paper, this girl had talent. He should have told her the truth, that she really had talent.

"It is excellent. Truly," was what he did say, moving away from it. "Better than anything I could have done. I'd like to have it, in fact. If I might."

"I-I...of course. Absolutely. Please, take it. I don't know what to say."

Then, he looked, really looked at her — the second thing he saw that night. And everything changed.

It wasn't that she was pretty. He knew that already. It wasn't that she was young. He also knew that. It wasn't that she could be easily pushed into being pliant, led to being eager concerning a quick affair with a famous artist. It, too, he knew by experience and simply looking at her.

But for the first time, Diego really saw her for what she was: a pretty, young girl who wanted nothing more in this world than for someone, anyone, to hold her hand, look her in the eye, and say that she was good enough, that she had it, that she was really, honestly, truly an artist, and could be a great one.

"You don't have to say anything," Diego said, grinning at her.

Wanting to be something. Wanting it more than anything in the world. Wanting to know that you are special, wanted, desired. It was something he knew all too well.

"You have true talent. Never forget that."

"T-thank you," she said, eyes softening with the proximity of tears.

"But I can't take this for free. Do you have a piece of paper I might have?"

"Certainly," she said.

She ran quickly towards the back of the gallery and picked up a large sketchpad she'd propped against the food table. Bringing it back, she presented it to him.

Art was his brother's domain, his brilliance blinding Diego from ever following. But just as he knew good art when he saw it, the elder brother also knew enough to be able to put a pencil to a pad, bring something out of it. It was not good, he knew that. But it was something he wanted to do for her, something he wanted Escobar, the great and famous painter, to do for her. Because it made him happy.

What to draw was a matter of convenience… the door to the gallery, in a few quick dashes of line. As he did it, he cursed himself for not being good enough, but he still didn't stop. As he did it, and felt frustration, he decided that he'd have to practice. Yes, practice.

Giving her the sketch, he accepted hers, an exchange that had both their eyes heavy with tears.

"Thank you," he managed to say as she presented it to him, wrapped in that day's newspaper.

About to shake her hand, he stopped, instead leaning forward to kiss her on the forehead. It was what Escobar would have done, he thought. No, that was not quite true. It was what the Escobar of her hopes and dreams would have done.

And what he would have said. So with the kiss, he left her one more gift before stepping out into the night.

"Always remember: it's not about what you do, but why you do it."

* * * *

Another night, another gallery. After that girl, it had all changed. No more hotel rooms or alleys. No more tears. No more bitterness.

Tonight's gallery was across the city, a tiny venue for big artistic dreams. The show, according to *Periscope*, began in a few hours. His disguise was perfected, the illusion as complete as he could make it. He'd better get moving.

But before he did, Diego paused and looked back over his shoulder, at the sketch hanging on his wall. A button missing from his uniform, a tiny apartment with crooked walls, even being the forgotten brother, none of it mattered. Tonight, he'd become Escobar, the famous painter, but not to seduce and ruin, or to steal a bit of his brother's success.

For them, for the hungry artists needing help, support, or just simple kindness like a kiss on the forehead, he'd be the Escobar of their dreams. That was his own great work.

All because of one young woman, the one who'd changed everything.

"Ciao, Madeline," he said, saluting the sketch she'd given him.

ABOUT THE AUTHOR

Calling M.Christian versatile is a tremendous understatement. Extensively published in science fiction, fantasy, horror, and even nonfiction, it is in erotica that M.Christian is widely considered an acknowledged master, appearing in multiple editions of *Best American Erotica*, *Best Gay Erotica*, *Best Lesbian Erotica*, *Best Bisexual Erotica*, *Best Fetish Erotica*, and many other magazines, sites, and anthologies.

In erotica, M.Christian's respected for their passionate imagination and chameleonic ability to convincingly write for — and as — a diverse range of gender expressions and sexual orientations.

Of their work, Tristan Taormino said, "M.Christian is a literary stylist of the highest caliber: smart, funny, frightening, sexy — there's nothing [they] can't write about… and brilliantly."

M.Christian's short fiction is collected in many bestselling books in a wide variety of genres, including the Lambda Award finalist *Dirty Words* and other queer collections such as *Filthy Boys* and *BodyWork*; erotic science fiction like *Rude Mechanicals*, *Technorotica*, *Better Than the Real Thing*, *Bachelor Machine*, *Skin Effect*, and *Hard Drive: The Best Sci-fi Erotica of M.Christian*.

As a novelist, M.Christian further demonstrates their versatility with the queer vampire novels, *Running Dry* and *The Very Bloody Marys*; the erotic romance, *Brushes*; the sensual cyberpunk, *Painted Doll*; and the controversial gay horror/thrillers *Finger's Breadth* and *Me2*.

On top of all that, they're prolific and anthologists, editing over twenty-five anthologies, namely the *Best S/M Erotica* series, *Pirate Booty*, *My Love For All That Is Bizarre: Sherlock Holmes Erotica*, *The Burning Pen*, *The Mammoth Book of Future Cops* and *The Mammoth Book of Tales of the Road* (with Maxim Jakubowski); and *Confessions, Garden of Perverse, Amazons* (with Sage Vivant), and others.

M.Christian is also a celebrated sexual futurist, through his novels and short stories as well as Senior Columnist and Managing Editor for *Future of Sex* (www.futureofsex.net), which provides "insights into the fascinating topic of the future of human sex and sexuality."

Visit www.mchristian.com for further information.

DO YOU WANT TO HELP PARISIAN PHOENIX OR ANY SMALL PUBLISHER OR INDEPENDENT AUTHOR?

- Buy books. Buy more books. Give books as gifts.
- Recommend authors to friends.
- Share Social Media Posts.
- Leave a review:
Amazon
Goodreads
Google Books
  - Readers use reviews to find books.
  - Retailers' web sites use reviews as part of their algorithm.
  - Some advertisers require a certain number of reviews.
- Join and share newsletters.
- Attend events.
- Join Goodreads and follow authors, mark their books as read, shelve and rate them.
- Check on Patreon and Kickstarter for the creators you love
- Start a book club.

Learn how

Subscribe to our Newsletter, "Bookish Babble", on

https://parisianphoenixpublishing.substack.com/

PARISIAN PHOENIX PUBLISHING KINK PRESENTS

JUICY BITS

Juicy Bits: Erotic Stories of BDSM, Kink & Fetish

From mild to wild—this book offers 25 erotic stories of BDSM, kink and fetish. Almost a dozen authors, from established voices in erotica to newcomers, fresh new characters to characters from existing fiction universes, these tales move the reader through a safe and consensual fantasies of exhibitionism, voyeurism, role play, sado-masochism, submission/dominance, impact play (and more) in labeled stories that allow the reader to explore the topics that intrigue them while skipping those that might be uncomfortable. Either way, the book provides a controlled, private opportunity to see what turns you on without taking your clothes off.

WRITING
DIRTY
WORDS
the not-so-sexy hustle of
making a living writing—
and the occasional crack of the whip
RALPH GRECO, JR.

www.ingramcontent.com/pod-product-compliance
Lightning Source LLC
Chambersburg PA
CBHW070510200726
48293CB00007B/2471